Hunted

Alycia Linwood

This is a work of fiction. Names, characters, places and incidents either are products of the author's imagination or are used fictitiously. Any resemblance to actual events or locales or persons, living or dead, is entirely coincidental.

Copyright © 2015 by Alycia Linwood

First Printing, 2015

Cover Stock Images Copyright: ©Canstockphoto.com

All rights reserved. No part of this novel may be reproduced, stored or transmitted in any form or by any means, electronic or mechanical, including photocopying, recording or by any information storage and retrieval system, without the prior permission in writing from the author.

ISBN-13: 978-1517449063
ISBN-10: 1517449065

I dedicate this book to my awesome readers. Thank you for your support! A big thanks to my beta readers and editors. I don't know what I would do without you all!

Chapter 1

I paced up and down the room, running a hand through my hair. Just before Lily was supposed to make an announcement and nicely explain the existence of tainted elementals to the public, a woman named Sophia Mornell cut into the transmission, presented tainted elementals as a threat, and told people to fight against us.

"What now?" I looked at Jaiden, who was sitting on the bed, his face serious.

"I don't know." He sighed. "I guess we'll find out soon."

I glanced at the TV screen but immediately had to look away because the news channel was still showing images of Jaiden and me. Jaiden had muted it when he could no longer stand to hear the reporters refer to us as a threat to mankind. "Who is she? What does she want?"

Jaiden just shook his head. "Someone who doesn't like tainted elementals."

"How did she even get all that footage?" I could understand that Sophia found videos of me going after

Blake because that had happened in the middle of the street. It had been impossible to control the observers and passersby, which was one of the reasons Lily had decided to reveal our secret.

But that didn't explain where Sophia had obtained the footage from Elemontera, the images of Jaiden killing people with his mind for his father, or the clips of me fighting in Elemontera. I couldn't imagine how Sophia could have gotten her hands on any of that.

"She has to be working with someone. Do you think your father has anything to do with it?" I asked.

A frown line creased Jaiden's brow. "My father?"

"Yeah. He escaped from that place where you kept him just in time. What if it was Sophia who freed him? If he or one of his scientists finally figured out how to turn regular adult elementals into tainted elementals, then maybe this is how they both planned to earn lots of money."

"I think I would know if he was working with her," Jaiden said. "She would have shown up somewhere or visited him, but I've never seen her before."

"Are you sure? You've been on Roivenna for a long time. Your father could have met with whoever he wanted and make God knows what kind of deals with them. And maybe Sophia finally completed his big plan and came for him." I put my hand on my hip, unsure how we were supposed to deal with this.

When I first found out about Jaiden's ability to mind-control people, I wasn't really thrilled about it. And after Blake successfully changed my whole life and made me believe things that weren't true, I convinced myself of how dangerous our abilities truly were. And for regular elementals who didn't even have the slightest chance of defending themselves against mind control, the news would be much harder to take in.

"Shit. You're right." Jaiden ran a hand across his face. "It's possible the two of them are working together, but why didn't they immediately announce their discovery?"

"Sophia doesn't seem like a stupid woman. If she immediately said she wanted to sell something, people would be suspicious of her intentions and maybe even blame her for creating such elementals. The news has to sink in first, and when the government and everyone confirms we were born like this because of genetic manipulation... then she can make her announcement or try to sell whatever product she wants." I didn't know if any other elementals had been turned into tainted after being born, like Jaiden. But it didn't really matter, because the majority were born like that.

"If my father is really working with her, then they could also be trying to sell the blockers. Maybe someone figured out how to configure them to defend people against most tainted elementals and not just against specific ones."

"We can drive ourselves crazy with theories." I stopped pacing and looked at him. "We should go find her."

He pressed his lips into a tight line, then his eyes fell onto the TV screen. "Every single cop is looking for us. We'll have to make ourselves invisible, and if they bring energy detectors..."

"Doesn't matter. We'll keep a low profile. Small spikes of energy can't be tracked." If Jaiden didn't want to use much of his energy because his elements were expiring and his father had run off with the serum that could restore them, then I could help him and keep him invisible with me. As long as he kept touching me, I was sure there wouldn't be any problems. Except that might cause a bigger spike of my energy, but wouldn't two tainted elementals flying together have a similar effect anyway?

The pocket of my jeans vibrated and I realized it was my phone. "Yeah?" I said tentatively, hoping no one from the press or the cops had gotten my number.

"Moira? Are you okay?" Noah's voice filled the line and my shoulders slumped in relief.

"Yeah, I'm fine. Did you..." I assumed there was no need to ask because probably everyone had seen the news. You'd have to live under a rock not to see it or hear about it from someone.

"Yeah, that was just... Did you talk to the cops to clear things up? Or ask Lily for advice?" he said, barely taking a breath.

"No. I don't want to go anywhere near the cops. They'd arrest us immediately, and who knows what would happen then?" We weren't in the times when threats like magic disease carriers were hunted down like animals or killed on the spot because someone suspected them of having committed a murder, but I wasn't about to risk it and find out. "And I couldn't reach Lily. She's probably overwhelmed by all the people who want to talk to her."

"But you were helping to save them from a psychopath, and all you did was either as an Elemontera agent or while you were trying to help others. They can't treat you like a criminal."

I noticed that he avoided mentioning Jaiden, but I wasn't about to bring him up. Noah and Jaiden's relationship was still too tense. And I didn't even want to think about how seeing Jaiden actually kill all those people affected Noah. I doubted it mattered to him that Jaiden hadn't had a choice.

"Yeah, and we might be able to prove that, but not now. Not while everyone is upset and scared…"

"So what are you going to do? Wait until things calm down?"

"No, Jaiden and I are going after Sophia."

"What?" Noah's voice was full of incredulity. "How do you even plan to find her? She might not even be in this city."

"She has to be somewhere around here." Why else would she say she cared about the city if she wasn't here to back up her claim? She probably knew the world would be in chaos and was waiting for an opportunity to come out with whatever she wanted to reveal next. "We think she might be working with Jaiden's father, especially since he's gone too and she has footage she shouldn't have."

"Um, have you considered the possibility that she's not working for anyone? She could be someone who lost a family member or someone she cared about because of tainted elementals," Noah said.

I thought about it for a moment. "Yeah, it could be that too." How could I not have considered that option? People who worked for Elemontera had families too. "Forget it. There are too many possibilities, but hacking into Lily's system and getting her hands on such information isn't the work of some random, grieving person."

"Yeah, someone is probably helping her." Noah sighed. "So... do you need some help?"

I didn't want Noah to risk his life. People would be looking for us and maybe he should stay in hiding until things calmed down, but tracking down Sophia on our own might take too much time. "Are you sure? We could always use some help, but... it's not safe."

Noah snorted. "Oh please. We've been in plenty of dangerous situations before. I can help."

"Okay, then come meet us at Harrlowe Factory. On the roof. Make sure no one sees you."

"I'll be there." The line went dead, and I slid the phone back into my pocket.

"Noah is coming to help us," I said.

"You shouldn't have told him where to meet us."

Jaiden got to his feet, crossing his arms. "Someone might be listening in."

"It's been what? A couple of hours? The cops and everyone is busy dealing with the news. I don't think they managed to find my number and immediately bugged the line." At least I hoped they couldn't. Briefly closing my eyes, I sighed. "But we should probably get rid of our phones and buy burners."

"Yeah." He stepped forward and pulled me into his arms, nuzzling my neck. "We'll need more help for this. Everyone will be looking for the two of us now that they've seen our faces, and I don't mean just the cops."

I placed my hands on his chest and looked up into his dark eyes. "Who else can we contact? I don't want to put anyone's life in danger."

"Their lives will be in danger if we don't find Sophia. If she has more footage from Elemontera and she shows it or twists it somehow to support her theory to prove that we're all dangerous..." He cleared his throat. "We could end up with angry masses after us, or even people who would want to use our abilities for their own benefit."

"Don't remind me." I let go of him and turned toward the window. One glance at the street didn't show signs that anything had changed, but I knew it had. There were fewer people outside, and those who were on the street were hurrying and kept glancing at passersby, probably wondering if an elemental with a mind-controlling ability was somewhere around them. Hell, maybe some of them even thought we could read minds. Not that I knew for sure none of us could do that. "Let's meet with Noah first and then we'll see what we can do. Maybe he can contact the others."

Jaiden nodded, and I turned myself into air, flying for the window that was slightly ajar.

Chapter 2

I rubbed my arms, suddenly feeling cold in the chilly twilight.

"Want my jacket?" Jaiden asked, but I shook my head.

A shimmering caught my attention and I pointed my finger toward it. "It's too big to be Noah."

"Looks like he brought company." Jaiden's brows were drawn together in concentration. "I recognize them. It's everyone from the hideout."

"But weren't they supposed to go home or wherever to live a happy life far from this drama?" One part of me was glad that I'd get to see everyone again, but by coming here they were putting their lives at risk.

"Um, they probably had to change their plans once the news leaked."

"Right." As we waited for our friends to land, I looked around to make sure nobody uninvited was coming. A gathering such as this must have caused a big energy spike and I hoped no one was monitoring us, or at least that people all over the city were upset enough to lose control of their elements and confuse the detectors.

Noah materialized first, his lips spreading into a smile when he saw me, his blue eyes kind and warm. "Hey, Moira." His gaze raked over Jaiden.

"So nice to see you all again," Marissa said as she appeared next to him, letting go of his hand. "I was hoping it would be under better circumstances, but whatever. I called Noah as soon as I could and he came for me and brought me here."

Nick became visible with Ashley and Sam, and Kenna landed not far from them, a scowl on her beautiful face.

"I didn't expect to see you all here." Especially not Kenna.

"We know elementals with stronger abilities would be more useful to you," Sam said. "But we came to help. Just because we can't fly or control people's minds doesn't mean we're useless."

"I'm really glad you're here." I pulled them all into hug, one by one, and waved at Kenna, who was keeping her distance.

"Let's go somewhere more private," Jaiden said, glancing nervously at the sky. "Someone could spot us here."

Everyone's heads turned toward me, and I realized they weren't really ready to follow Jaiden's orders again. "Good idea. Come on. There's an empty apartment in the building across from here with a nice fire escape that we can use in case we need it."

Noah shrugged. "Sounds good to me. But can't we just grab everyone and fly out? Our abilities are even better now. Isn't that right, Nick?"

Nick bobbed his head. "Yep."

"So you basically just came to show off." A grin formed on my lips.

"Nah." Nick waved his hand, but his blue eyes were filled with amusement. "Well, maybe a little."

"Then let's hope that if someone comes to try and capture us, they don't have any blocking devices," I said, then turned to Ashley and Marissa, who were walking next to me as we made our way to the roof door. "So what do you think about Sophia's announcement?"

"Do you have any idea who she could be?" Marissa's gray eyes narrowed. "I swear she couldn't have picked a worse moment. How did she even know Lily was planning to make an announcement?"

"We don't really know anything about her," I said. "But we'll find out."

"I still don't get why she'd wage a war on us. We're more powerful. We'd win," Nick said confidently.

"Are you sure about that?" Sam asked. "There's more of them and not that many of us. Besides, some of us are only as powerful as element preservers."

"Do you think preservers could side with regulars?" Ashley's green eyes went wide. "But they were in our situation once! All magic disease carriers were persecuted. Do you really think they'd just decide we should all be killed or something because some of us are more powerful?"

"I hope not." Marissa said. "I don't want to think our world could regress."

"We could just hand over the mind controllers," Kenna said, flipping her dark brown hair over her shoulder, and everyone's gazes snapped toward her. "What? Oh come on. Don't look at me like that. Sophia used the two of them for a reason." She bobbed her head toward Jaiden and me. "What people are truly afraid of is mind control and killing with a single thought. Stronger elements, flying, and invisibility... bah, who cares about that? It's not that different from regular elements, but mind control..."

"Kenna..." Nick said, a pinched expression on his face. "Didn't we agree that if you came here, you'd behave?"

"I'm just telling the truth, brother." She gave him a nonchalant look. "If it weren't for mind abilities, we wouldn't have any trouble. I was stuck in that underground rat-infested place because of that bastard." She pointed at Jaiden. "And now we're most likely going to be hunted down because he and his girlfriend killed people with their minds. Can't you see? It's all because of them."

"Don't forget who helped you get off the island." Nick groaned. "Maybe I should've left you there."

"Hey!" Kenna's mouth twisted. "I wouldn't have needed help if it hadn't been for..."

"Yeah, yeah, let's not talk about that right now," Noah said, flailing his hands.

We descended through a dark, empty stairway, and I was glad the building was an abandoned factory because we were way too loud. "What we need to focus on is finding Sophia. Who knows what else she's planning to do? Now that's she got everyone's attention I'm sure she'll resurface and try to convince people that elementals like us all pose a threat."

"Great. Just what we needed." Kenna huffed.

"You don't have to be here," Nick said, folding his arms across his chest. "I shouldn't have told you anything."

"Nuh uh. I'm staying," Kenna said. "I won't leave you alone with them. Who knows what stupid idea they'll put you up to?"

"I don't need protection." Nick frowned.

"Doesn't mean I won't have to keep an eye on you," she replied.

We emerged into an alley full of trash, and I almost stepped into a puddle of some disgusting orange liquid. Dodging the cans and papers, I dashed to the door of an old apartment building.

"Shh." I raised my finger in front of my lips and waited until I was sure everyone was quiet. "Some older people still live here, so let's not draw their attention, okay?"

Everyone nodded, and we slowly and carefully climbed the old stairs until we reached the highest floor where no one was supposed to be living. Jaiden busted the old knob off and we entered a room that smelled of dust and mold.

Kenna screwed up her nose. "You brought us here? Really? Couldn't we just go somewhere nicer?"

"No, this a good place," I said. "Plenty of exits, not many people, and we can still check if someone is following us. If they show up around here, then we'll be sure."

"If you say so." Kenna dusted off one of the chairs and gingerly took a seat, careful of her dark blue jeans.

When everyone settled onto the old couch and sofas, I brought a wooden chair next to Jaiden's and took a seat. "There's something I wanted to suggest before all the drama with Sophia started..." I glanced at Jaiden, who took my hand into his and squeezed gently. "My grandfather left me some money and... I wanted to create a group for tainted elementals. Something like Lily's organization but led by tainted elementals and not by someone who might not have our best interest at heart all the time. Lily has done a lot, but... she's not one of us."

"Well, I like the idea, but right now..." Noah grimaced.

"No," Marissa interrupted. "It's an excellent idea. Tainteds need all the support they can get, now more than ever. I'm sure many of them out there don't know what to do, especially those who don't know anyone like them or who are trying to pretend they are regulars."

"Tainteds? Is that what we're calling ourselves now?" Ashley scowled.

"I heard it on the news earlier today." Marissa shrugged.

"Doesn't matter," Sam said, clasping his hands in his lap. "If we form a group now, do you think anyone will want to contact us? How would we make sure our enemies don't hunt us down? Hell, I'm not even sure who our enemies are at the moment. The cops? People? Sophia?"

Kenna scoffed, her eyes boring into mine. "No one will ever follow you. Not after they've seen what you can do."

"I wasn't intending on leading the organization myself," I said. "No one would know I'm funding it or anything. Just you guys."

Noah ran a hand through his black hair. "So the group would operate in secret, right? We'd gather as many tainteds as we can and try to help them."

"Yeah, that was the idea." I intertwined my fingers with Jaiden's. His warm touch managed to keep away the cold dread filling my stomach. "We could still try. Maybe the government will think this through better and they'll actually let us voice our opinions on the whole thing. They can't just decide to kill us all. Most of tainteds are just teenagers. They can't kill off everyone whose genes were manipulated before birth. And what about the younger generations? Some of the tainteds are too young to use their elements."

"Okay," Noah said. "I guess we could start a support group, or whatever we're going to call it, and see what happens."

"Who would be the leader?" Nick asked.

"Um, I don't know," I said. "Maybe we could vote."

"Noah," Ashley and Marissa said at the same time, and Noah's eyebrows shot up.

"Why me?" he asked.

"You're the best for that kind of thing," Marissa said.

"I am?" Noah gave everyone a bewildered look, but no one protested the idea.

"If you want to do it, I don't see any problems," I said. "I think you'd be good at it."

"Okay then." He raised his chin up, widening his shoulders, and then frowned at me. "Wait, what am I supposed to do? Just look for tainteds and ask them to join the club?"

"You can offer them your help so they can understand their abilities better or just talk with them about their troubles." The truth was, I hadn't really thought that far. I'd always assumed the elementals who needed something would contact us. Granted, that would work in a world where Sophia's announcement hadn't happened. "I know it'll be hard to get them to trust us, but... you're charming enough. You'll figure something out."

"Thanks a lot." He rolled his eyes. "I guess I'll have to improvise then. But you realize that this is different from just recruiting people like I was doing while..." His eyes flickered to Jaiden, and his jaw clenched. "Well, you know."

"Yeah, I get it," I said. Jaiden's little group had been mostly in hiding and safe on Roivenna, and in the city there would be constant danger. Noah couldn't pick a building where he could regularly meet with other elementals without risking being seen. Except... "Are those underground tunnels monitored? You could take elementals there to train them or to talk."

"Maybe. I don't know. I'll have to check." Noah took a deep breath.

"What about the rest of us?" Nick asked.

"You could go talk to Lily," I said. "I'm afraid reaching out to her over the phone would be a bad idea, and if Jaiden or I go there, she might not have a choice but to report us to the cops. You could ask her if she knows anything about Sophia."

"I can do that." Nick tilted his head back.

"Nick, I'm going with you," Kenna said.

"Okay, you two go see Lily, and..." I looked at Sam, Ashley, and Marissa, who were all carefully watching me. None of them had an air element, so doing anything that required a quick escape was out of the question. "And you three... you're going to be our eyes and ears out there. Since you can pass for regular elementals because no one has seen you, you can check what people are doing and thinking about us, then report to Noah."

They all nodded.

"And what are you going to do?" Marissa asked, concern filling her eyes.

"Jaiden and I are going to see what we can uncover about Sophia. We have a few theories about her that we need to check," I said, then focused on Nick. "Talk to Lily as soon as possible. If she knows something..."

"What are you going to do when you find that woman?" Ashley asked. "Mind-control her not to be against us?" Her voiced faltered. "Kill her?"

I licked my lips. "No, I hope we won't have to do any of that. Actually, we should try not to be the monsters everyone thinks we are. She probably has a secret agenda, and if we figure out what it is, we can show the world that she's not really concerned about people's well-beings."

"And what if she is?" Sam asked.

I doubted that was a possibility, because why go through all the trouble of obtaining the footage and hacking Lily's transmission? "If she is... well, we'll deal with that somehow."

"Okay, so let's go." Nick jumped to his feet and Kenna followed, curling her lip as she inspected her jeans for any stains.

"Be careful," I said. "Make sure no one sees you leaving here together."

Everyone got to their feet except Jaiden and me, and after everyone said their goodbyes, I turned toward him and tilted my head.

"So where do we look first?" I asked.

"Elemontera... or what's left of it."

Chapter 3

"I don't remember any of this," I said as Jaiden and I landed in the backyard of a small house. Unless bits of my memory were still missing after Blake had messed with my mind, I had never been here before. The house looked like any family house down this street. Its facade was perfectly white, the blinds drawn, and the porch filled with pots of flowers that were hiding two garden gnomes.

"That's because you haven't been here before," Jaiden said, going for the front door.

"Is this someone's house?" Maybe he'd brought me to talk to one of Elemontera's former employees or something.

"It used to be Elemontera's." A frown creased his brow as he studied the door. "Someone got here before us."

"How do you...?" I came closer and saw the knob was broken. "Are you sure it wasn't Lily's men?" I assumed they would have checked any properties that were connected to Elemontera after the headquarters were shut down.

He shook his head. "Lily doesn't know about this."

"Oh." My eyebrows shot up. "And you never thought you could mention it to her because...?"

"I had my reasons." He pushed the door open, taking a peek inside.

"Who else knows about this place?" I asked as we entered the darkness, and Jaiden immediately flipped the switch, lighting up the hallway. Since he knew exactly where to find the switch, I assumed that meant he'd been here more than once.

"My father and a few of his confidants." He inspected a room that looked like a regular kitchen. To our right was a bathroom, and it didn't look like it had been disturbed either, so we continued down the hallway until we reached a large bookshelf.

"Let me guess. Something is behind that." I pointed at the shelf.

"Yeah." Jaiden skimmed over the books until he found the right one and pulled it out. As he pushed his hand through the opening, something crunched behind the shelf, which started to move until it slid completely to the side, revealing a door with a keypad.

"That's a lot of protection," I said as Jaiden punched in the code, and the door finally opened. "What's supposed to be inside?"

"Come and see." He pushed the door wide open and let me enter a small room crammed with shelves and papers.

"Um, great. A ton of papers. Why is any of this important?" I picked up one of the files hoping it might contain Jack's old research that could help us recreate the serum Jaiden needed to keep his elements, but all the paper consisted of was a list of names. At least I thought they were names.

"Oh, that thing you're holding isn't important at all. Just like most of things in here. It's just trash." A smile tugged at Jaiden's lips as he went to the corner of the room and picked up a stack of papers.

"What?" I gaped at him. "Is it more protection? For what?" That seemed like a lot of trouble to go through to hide something. Jaiden finally picked up a small metal box and fiddled with the tiny lock on it until it opened. I loomed over him, trying to see what was inside. Jaiden swore as we both realized the box was empty.

"What was supposed to be inside?" Judging by the worried look on Jaiden's face, it was something valuable.

"A flash drive. With most of Elemontera's files from earlier days. It's a backup of a backup in case everything else fails. Someone has taken it." He got to his feet and threw the box against the wall, causing a loud racket. "We could've used it to check if Sophia was mentioned somewhere in there."

"Do you think it was stolen?" Thieves usually didn't bother to put everything back into place after they found what they were looking for. I mean, wasting time on rearranging things surely wouldn't be easy and they would mostly likely get caught before they were done. "Was it your father?"

"I don't know." He rubbed his chin. "I guess it was him or everything would be... a mess."

"Except he wouldn't have to break in."

"Yeah." Jaiden pressed his lips into a tight line. A sound of a door opening somewhere in the hallway made us look at each other. I just stood there, motionless, trying to hear the sound again, but everything was quiet. A shimmering thread rose from Jaiden's body and slipped through the crack in the door.

"Shit! Someone's here!" a panicked male voice yelled, and Jaiden and I burst through the door. I rose my fiery hands up, ready to throw a fireball at the intruder. A dark-eyed girl yelped when she saw us, pressing herself closer to the guy, who was gaping at us.

"Please don't hurt us!" The guy lifted his hands up, moving forward so he'd shield the girl. "We don't mean any trouble."

"Who are you? What are you doing here?" Jaiden's voice was tense, and a shimmering thread shot for the guy's head. I pulled my fire back and placed my hand on Jaiden's arm, shaking my head, and he gave me a long look before he called his air back. We didn't immediately have to jump into someone's mind and force them to tell us things.

"I... My name is Kyle," the guy said. "This is my sister, Willa."

"You're tainted elementals," I said. Kyle had yelled when he saw Jaiden's shimmering thread, so he had to be one of us.

"No, we..." Kyle stammered.

Willa, who was almost a head shorter than him, slapped him on the arm and narrowed her eyes at him. "Oh, stop it, K. They're like us."

"What?" He stared at her for a moment, then blinked at Jaiden and me. "Oh, right. The shimmering..."

"What are you doing here?" Jaiden asked.

"We... we thought no one lived here because we haven't see anyone for days, so we thought we could... Never mind." Kyle placed his hands on his sister's shoulders and tried to steer her to the door. "We're leaving. We'll find another place. Sorry to disturb you."

"Wait." Willa dug in her heels. "It's them! They were on the news!"

"Shh." Kyle hissed, grabbing her hand and bolting for the door. But before they could get out, Jaiden created a wall of air in front of them, and they couldn't cross through no matter how hard they tried. I glanced at Jaiden's expressionless face and noticed beads of sweat appearing on his forehead.

"We're not going to hurt you. We just want to talk," I said.

"Please let us go. We won't tell anyone we saw you." Kyle said. "I promise."

"You're lying," Jaiden said through his teeth, and this time his shimmering thread jumped for Kyle so fast no one had a chance to stop it. "Why are you here?" Jaiden asked with all the intensity in the world.

"We're here to watch the house in case Maiers' son or anyone else appears," Kyle said, his eyes glazed.

"Who sent you?" Jaiden asked.

"Jack Maiers."

"When did you last speak to my father?"

"Two days ago. He promised a safe place for me and my sister if we did what he asked."

Willa gaped at her brother, probably not comprehending why he was saying all that. She visibly swallowed as her eyes fell on Jaiden.

"How did you meet him?"

"He caught us here when he came for something and said this was his house, but that we could stay if we..."

"Yeah, yeah, heard it already." Jaiden pulled his element back, his jaw set. But if his father had been here for the flash drive, that meant he was probably trying to rebuild Elemontera somewhere else. Lovely.

"Why didn't you come for the drive before?" I turned to Jaiden.

"I thought I would be able to catch him here, but after what happened... I forgot." He rubbed his forehead. "Will you do it or should I?"

"Do what?" I frowned as I followed his gaze to Kyle and Willa. Oh, right, make them forget they'd ever seen us. Except... "Why would your father leave them here to watch the house if he knew you could just mind-control them to forget?"

"Maybe he wasn't expecting me." A frown creased Jaiden's brow.

"But who then? Lily? She could bring mind controllers with her too. And why would he watch the house if he already got what he wanted?" I doubted there was anything in here more valuable than the missing flash drive. "If there isn't anything else in here...?"

Jaiden blinked in confusion. "I don't know. It's strange."

"Yes, it is." I focused on Kyle and Willa. "Where is your family? Why did you need a safe place to stay?"

"We..." A huge wave of water rose toward Jaiden and me, and I sent a blast of my air in its direction to destroy it. While I was shielding my eyes from thousands of drops of water that were flying everywhere, I glimpsed Kyle and Willa running away.

"Oh, no you don't." I turned into air and rushed after them. But as I emerged onto the street, I couldn't see anything. Materializing, I squinted my eyes, trying to spot the shimmering. Jaiden appeared next to me, his eyes flashing with anger.

"Do you see them?" I asked.

"No." His air surged out and started circling around the houses, but I knew it would be impossible to catch them now that we'd lost them.

"Well, the worst that can happen is that they tell your father or someone else that they saw us, which doesn't really matter." I shrugged.

"True, but I want to know who my father was expecting to show up here."

"Me too." The distinct sound of a police siren could be heard not far from us. "We should get out of here. Any other places your father used to hide his important things?"

"Not really. Lily took almost everything."

"So the only thing we can do is wait for Nick to tell us what Lily found out." I groaned. All these special abilities we had and there was not much we could do. Awesome.

"Maybe there's something else." The corners of Jaiden's lips turned up. "The cops are supposed to work with Lily, but who says they'll give her all the information? Maybe we should check for ourselves and see what they've got on Sophia."

"Okay. Do you know a high ranking cop and where to find them? Because I'm not about to parade right in front of people who are looking for me." The cops were mostly powerless against us, but now that everyone knew the truth, maybe they had found a way to detect our presence or were being more careful, and I didn't want to risk that.

"Yeah, I do. I just hope he still lives at the same place. He knows my father."

"A shady cop? Sure. Let's check." We both turned invisible and soared into the sky.

Chapter 4

"Is that him?" I whispered as Jaiden and I crouched behind one of the low stone walls. Across the street was a tall building with a white facade ornamented with flowery symbols. In front of the big door stood a man in a dark suit and white gloves, and he was talking to a dark-haired guy dressed in dark blue jeans and a black hoodie. The hoodie guy was probably the one we were looking for, although he looked terribly out of place in front of that building.

"Yeah." Jaiden turned invisible, so I did the same, and we carefully crossed the street. People might not be able to see us, but they could certainly run us over if we weren't careful, and I didn't want to risk having to squeeze myself under a speeding car, and flying too high might catch the attention of other taianteds, which we didn't want.

As we were nearing the hoodie guy, he nodded at the man at the door and slipped inside. Jaiden and I followed. I was glad the door was still slightly ajar, so we could drift inside without having to wait for someone to push the door open.

Sure, we could turn visible or use our air on the door, but if we did the former, the guard wouldn't let us in, unless we mind-controlled him. And if we did the latter, the guy would think we were ghosts. Well, maybe not, but it would certainly catch his attention and we couldn't afford that.

We entered the lobby. There was a red carpet on the floor, and a few black sofas and tables on one side. Behind them was a stairway and an elevator. The hoodie guy went to the elevator, but it closed before we could reach him, so we waited until we could see which floor he stopped on.

Once we were sure he would be somewhere on the sixth floor, Jaiden and I hastened toward the stairway and did a dizzying flight until we reached the right floor. My blood spiking with adrenaline, I slowed my air and looked up and down the hallway. A rich gray carpet covered the floor, and there were four doors, all identical. Jaiden went toward the closest one, probably inspecting the number on it. His shimmery hand waved at me, and I floated closer.

"He's here," Jaiden said. "Looks like we can squeeze through the door."

"Great," I mumbled as his air sort of melted under the door. I wasn't thrilled about having to jumble my whole body so I could push myself through the opening, but I gritted my invisible teeth and slipped through the small crack, feeling as if my whole body was being reassembled.

Fighting the urge to sigh in relief when I spread out my air again, I looked up and saw Jaiden's cloud shimmering not far from the guy, who was now taking off his hoodie, revealing a black t-shirt. We had to stop him before he started to take off anything else.

"Hello, Warren," Jaiden said, materializing behind the guy, who immediately gasped. His hand went for the back of his pants and he drew a gun. Warren's green eyes were wide, his chest heaving as he pointed the weapon at Jaiden, who only smirked at him. For some reason, I'd assumed Warren would be older, maybe in his forties or closer to Jack's age, but now I could see that he was in his thirties.

"Oh, come on. Move that little thingy out of my face," Jaiden said in a bored voice.

"What are you doing here?" Warren asked, but didn't lower the gun.

"We have some questions for you," I said, becoming visible. Warren turned the gun toward me, then back at Jaiden, unsure of where to aim.

"Drop the gun. We're not going to hurt you." Jaiden crossed his arms.

"Yeah, am I really supposed to trust you two?" Warren's lip curled, but he finally lowered the gun, probably realizing that he'd only get tired if he kept it up. We could take the gun from him in under a second. "Everyone is looking for you. In fact, I should call the chief and alert him..."

"But you're not going to do that, are you?" Jaiden snickered. "Not unless you want us to get mad, and then your coworkers could find out interesting things about your dedication to your job or... the lack of it."

"What do you want?" Warren kept eyeing Jaiden and me, slowly backing against the wall so he could keep us both in sight.

"Sophia Mornell," I said. "What do you know about her?"

"She's that woman who exposed who you truly are to the world," he said, and looked pretty satisfied about it. "Why do you think I know anything about her?"

"You have access to certain files," Jaiden said, taking a menacing step forward. "So tell me, what do the cops have on her?"

"Nothing." He gritted his teeth, throwing the gun onto the table and clenching his fingers.

"Don't lie to me. There has to be something." Jaiden's hand flickered in and out of visibility.

"There was," Warren said. "But it was deleted. Someone with a very high clearance did it, because there's absolutely no trace of any data about her, not even her basic info."

"Don't you have any backups or anything she couldn't have deleted?" I asked. It didn't look like he was lying, and if Sophia could break into Lily's systems and avoid her protection, then she could do the same to the cops.

"No. Well, she doesn't seem to have any criminal record, so there aren't any physical files about her." He ran a hand through his short light brown hair.

"What about other files? Surely she went to a doctor or to school or something," I said. Someone had to know something, unless she had drastically changed her appearance and her name.

"We're looking, but so far we haven't got anything." Warren's shoulders slumped. "It's possible she's using a fake name or has made sure no one can recognize her."

"Great." I shook my head. "Did you get any other footage of her? Run her face for any matches on surveillance cameras?"

"Yeah, but we got no results. Either she's moving where no one can see her or she's getting help from one of your kind." He sneered. "You really think you're ruling the world, don't you? Invisibility and all?"

"What about my father?" Jaiden asked. "Seen him lately?"

Warren went perfectly still, his face expressionless. "Not really. Why? Can't you find your own father? Why don't you just call him? Ah, wait." A smile spread across Warren's lips. "Is he not taking your calls?"

Jaiden turned invisible and materialized with his hand around Warren's throat, shoving him against the wall. Warren's eyes bulged, and he spluttered as he tried to pry

Jaiden's fingers off. I was thinking about intervening when Jaiden dropped Warren and took a step back.

"Don't push my patience," Jaiden said coldly. "You know what I'm capable of."

"I do." A shadow crossed Warren's face.

"I'm not going to ask again," Jaiden said as Warren straightened his back and massaged his neck.

"All I know is that your father is still in the city. One of the surveillance cameras caught him near the bridge, but we lost him later," he said, glaring at Jaiden. "You can check my mind if you want. I'm telling the truth."

"Thank you for your cooperation," Jaiden said with a smile. "I'm sure you'll be smart enough to keep your mouth shut about our little chat."

"I won't say anything." Warren looked at me. "But if I see you when I'm on duty, I won't let you go."

"As if you could ever catch us." Jaiden snorted.

"Oh, believe that as much as you want," Warren said. "By running away from the cops, who, by the way, only want to question you and get your side of the story for their investigation, you're only confirming Sophia's words. But I guess two criminals like you know that you're guilty, so that's why you can't let anyone catch you."

"That's none of your business," I said, then met Jaiden's eyes. We should be getting out of here. The longer we stayed, the bigger the chances Warren had something on him that could alert the cops to come after us. Sure, maybe he wasn't stupid enough to risk our wrath but if he knew he could get away with it... "Jaiden."

"Let's go." Jaiden turned into a shimmering cloud, and I did the same. As we disappeared through the hole under the door, a strange feeling of dread filled my stomach. This was all wrong. We should be trying to discredit Sophia's story and not helping her, but first we had to find her and stop her from doing more damage.

"This is so not helping," I said. "Sophia has too many connections in high places if she could get all the info scrubbed as if it never existed."

"Maybe there's another way to stop her," Jaiden said as we flew toward the roof. Going out this way seemed like a better idea than going back through the main door. Another tainted elemental could spot us if we emerged onto the street, and if Warren's suspicion that Sophia was working with one of us was true, then we had even more problems. But why would one of us be helping her? Unless she threatened them somehow or promised them protection of some kind.

"Do you have any ideas?" I whizzed past the stairway.

"I could turn myself in and explain that you were acting against your will," he said.

"What?" I nearly slammed into the wall. "Absolutely not. Are you out of your fucking mind?"

"I killed those people, Moira. You... you killed in self-defense, to protect the others, and when you couldn't control yourself. And I..."

"No. You were acting on your father's orders."

"Yeah, but I had a choice. I didn't have to do it." He materialized and stopped in the middle of the roof.

"And what would he have done if you hadn't? He'd find another way to kill them and hurt you." I turned visible and placed my hand on his cheek. His dark eyes were restless as he looked at me, his shoulders curling. "You told me they weren't all innocent people."

He bent his head. "Yeah, but... I shouldn't have... I shouldn't have done it." He pulled away from my touch and turned his back to me.

"Turning yourself in to the cops won't change the past." I raised my voice. "We did what we did. We can't go back and do differently, but we can do something good with our powers. We're some of the most powerful tainteds out there, and if someone can find and stop Sophia, it's us. She's not only accusing us of being murderers. If she were, things would be simple, but she's blaming everyone and claiming we're all the same, and if one of us gets arrested, I'm sure she'll come out with some proof or use something against us. We can't win this until we know who we're dealing with. If her connections are that good, many people will be in danger."

He faced me, a frown creasing his brow. "Maybe you're right. I just... I've been feeling strange lately. Like my head is going to explode or something."

I took a step toward him. "It's your elements, isn't it? You know they're expiring and it's making you anxious."

"I guess." He licked his lips. "I don't know. With Sophia and my father missing, and that footage... it brings back bad memories."

"What happens when your elements weaken? Would you just lose them forever or something?" I wasn't sure how the serum worked exactly.

"I... I lose my ability to use them. I've never had to go without the serum long enough for them to completely drain, so I don't know what happens." He took a deep breath and placed his arms around my waist, tugging me toward him so our noses almost touched. "It doesn't matter. Let's hope Lily has better luck. She's resourceful."

"Yeah." My lips parted and I looked up at him, then pressed my mouth against his. Slipping my fingers through his dark brown hair, I deepened the kiss. When we broke apart, a smile spread across my face. "I have an idea. Let's forget all this drama for a moment."

Jaiden's eyebrows rose up.

"Come on." I grabbed his hand and turned us both into air. We flew to the other side of the city, and I didn't stop until we were at the top of a clock tower. Materializing right under the clock, we settled on a stone windowsill. I dangled my feet over the edge and watched the city as it sank into the darkness, the flashy lights blinking everywhere. A small smile appeared on Jaiden's lips and I leaned my head against his shoulder, and he wrapped his arm around me.

"It's beautiful, isn't it?" I asked, glad that we didn't have to be afraid we'd lose our balance and fall to our deaths. At least that was a nice, useful, non-dangerous perk of our abilities.

"Yeah," he said, planting a soft kiss onto my hair. We sat there watching the sky and forgetting our worries for a couple of hours.

Chapter 5

The next morning my phone rang, rousing me from my sleep. I felt across my nightstand for the phone and nearly shoved the lamp and glass of water off it. Blindly pressing the answer button, I put the phone against my ear. "Yeah?"

"Moira, hey, it's me," Marissa said. "Are you up?"

"I'm still in bed. Why?" I pushed myself up on my elbows, glancing at Jaiden, who stirred next to me. We'd found an empty hotel room last night and fallen asleep almost immediately. Flying around like a crazy person could be exhausting.

"Turn on the TV. There's a debate going on," she said. "Something like a pro- and anti-tainteds campaign. You wanted to know how people would react, and I think that's the closest we've got."

"Okay, thanks." I looked around the room for a remote, glad that we'd picked a decent hotel that had a functioning television.

"Talk to you later," Marissa said and ended the call. Placing the phone back on the nightstand, I spotted the remote across the room and used my air to toss it onto the bed.

"What are you doing?" Jaiden asked, stretching out, his hair disheveled. "Want to watch morning cartoons?"

"No matter how much I'd like to watch cartoons, that's not it. Marissa told me they were discussing tainteds on one of the channels." I turned on the TV, realizing Marissa hadn't told me which channel, but I assumed I'd find it easily enough. If the topic was so important, it wouldn't be on some random entertainment channel.

Jaiden sat up, running both of his hands through his hair, a frown creasing his brow. "This should be interesting."

"Yeah." I flipped through the channels until I found the right one. Two women were sitting in a small, light blue studio. The blonde had her arms clasped in her lap, her face serious, her hazel eyes intent on her interviewer, who had long curly dark hair and big dark brown eyes rimmed with kohl.

"So you're saying it's our fault we manipulated our children's genes in hopes they wouldn't inherit the disease or weak elements?" the dark-haired woman asked.

"No, Ella, that's not even close to what I'm saying." The blonde pressed her red lips into a tight line. "The genetic manipulation is responsible for creating this new type of elemental, but I'm not saying it's necessarily a bad thing. We wanted to eradicate magic disease and have stronger elements, like you said, and look, we have that. These tainted elementals have very strong elements and they don't have the disease. And apparently carriers can't feel their elements either."

"But there was a case of one tainted elemental who had the disease, or at least that's what the latest reports are claiming."

"It could be true, but it appears that the elemental was infected later and not born with the disease."

Someone must have leaked that info about Blake, because I couldn't imagine Lily doing that, or maybe she'd had no choice since someone had gotten the footage of Blake displaying abilities that didn't belong to carriers or element preservers.

"I'm still not convinced that's a good thing." Ella shook her head. "The abilities they have are... too much. I mean, anyone can mind-control you or kill you... That's... I'm sorry, but that's terrifying. Aren't you afraid for your life?"

"I know there's some footage about special abilities that could pose a threat to people, but we've been living with tainted elementals without knowing it and didn't notice any problems or drastic increase in crime. They're just powerful teenagers. Just because they have these abilities doesn't mean they're going to use them to hurt anyone or do bad things," the blonde said. "How many elementals have strong abilities and could use them for nefarious deeds? But they don't do it, because they're good, decent people. Magic disease carriers were once considered such a threat, but look at them now. Most of them can lead normal and happy lives in a way that is safe for everyone. We shouldn't persecute or marginalize those children just because their elements are stronger than ours."

"But how can you know you weren't mind-controlled to think this? And why wouldn't they use those abilities if they could? I can imagine myself mind-controlling my way out of trouble or to get what I want." A ghost of a smile traced Ella's lips. "In fact, I saw a perfect pair of shoes yesterday. Really expensive. Imagine if I had the ability to fly inside and take them without being seen. Why wouldn't I do that? Tell me, Miranda. Wouldn't you at least be tempted?"

"Actually," Miranda said. "You could walk into that shop in a mask and threaten the sales lady with your element, rip out the camera, and run away. Or you could take a gun. Why not? Then you can protect yourself with the help of carriers, who can sense if the cops with elements are coming."

Ella frowned, looking uncertain for a moment.

"Bad people will always find a way to do bad things, but that doesn't mean every kid with powerful elements will use them to commit crimes. Imagine what we could do with the help of tainted elementals. We could save people's lives if those elementals who can fly decide to help. What we should be doing is showing those kids how to be decent people, and not reject them and force them to act against us," Miranda said. "We can't treat them as if they were some abominations that shouldn't have been created. They don't have any fault in what's going on, and many of them only have more than one element and their abilities aren't different from those of element preservers or regular elementals. If we judge everyone for crimes of one person, then we might as well condemn ourselves because there are killers among us too."

"What about Moira Arnolds and Jaiden Maiers?" Ella suddenly asked, and I flinched. "Are we supposed to accept that they couldn't help who they are, so they ended up killing people with their minds?"

"It hasn't been confirmed yet that they can do that."

"But if they can? Those videos look very real to me."

"If it's all real, then there should be an investigation, and they should be tried like any other person in such a situation."

I swallowed hard and glanced at Jaiden, whose face was completely expressionless.

"And if there are more elementals as powerful as them? If they wipe our minds or force us to do God knows what?" Ella persisted.

"From what I've heard, mass mind control would be hard and it's possible to notice something is wrong and realize your mind has been tampered with, which would then unravel most of the mind control."

"But if they force us to kill each other or hurt our families, and we couldn't fight them off... what's the point if we realize later what we've done?"

"There's no reason to panic," Miranda said, raising her hand. "Everyone is thinking the worst of these elementals just because they've seen two of them do something bad. I know it's scary that someone could control our minds or kill us with one thought, but there are other ways of forcing people to do things... blackmail, drugs, threats... and we have elements and weapons... That makes all of us dangerous. We shouldn't be on a hunt for innocent teenagers. We should catch those who make trouble and violate the laws, but let's treat everyone like human beings."

Ella chewed on her lower lip, probably trying to come up with something to say. Miranda had valid points. If someone wanted to do bad things, they could.

"Those special abilities do make it harder to catch and find the real perpetrator," Miranda continued. "But that doesn't mean it's impossible. I heard the police can already track the elemental energy of tainted elementals and find them."

"Well, they haven't really had luck with Moira and Jaiden, have they?" Ella all but whooped in delight over her bright idea.

"Not yet, but I'm sure they'll find them. In many cases the perpetrators aren't found immediately. It takes some time, but it'll be solved," Miranda said confidently.

"If you say so." Ella gave her a condescending smile. "I'll be praying for the day when they invent blockers so that no one can enter my mind."

Miranda just glared at her.

Jaiden sighed, and I focused my attention on him.

"The government still hasn't given any official statements, have they?" I asked.

"I don't think so," he said. "They would be having a different kind of a debate right now if they'd done it."

"Right." I looked back at the screen. Ella had gotten to her feet and was pointing at the big display behind her.

"Let's see what the public says." A graph appeared behind her, filling the whole screen. "Seventy-eight percent admit they aren't entirely comfortable around those new elementals, two percent are indifferent, and only twenty percent feel safe and don't think this changes anything." Ella's triumphant face came into view. "See? People aren't that fast to agree with you, Miranda."

"It's normal that they're scared of the unknown, but once they realize their children, neighbors, and friends are tainted elementals, that they haven't known it, and that everything is the same, they'll accept it," Miranda said. "As long as people like Sophia Mornell are trying to spread fear, things won't get better."

"I wouldn't say Ms. Mornell is trying to spread fear," Ella said. "She warned us about a very potent threat, and maybe even saved our lives. Who knows what those two elementals would've done if they hadn't been discovered? People who knew about this would've kept it a secret for God knows how long, and we'd continue with genetic manipulation, unaware of the danger."

"Please tell me you're not suggesting that people should stop genetic manipulation and that we go back to having high rates of magic disease and weak elements." Miranda gaped at her. "You can't possibly think that magic disease carriers are less dangerous than tainted elementals. Would you rather live surrounded by people who might lose control of themselves and go for your element, or by tainted elementals who don't have any reasons to harm you?"

"I can use an element-blocking bracelet, thank you very much," Ella said. "And against tainteds, what am I going to use? I can only hope I don't cross their path."

"And what about our water and energy supplies? Did you forget we have those only because we're taking elemental energy from people with pure elements? Not every genetic manipulation results in tainted elements. Many actually end up creating a pure element that we need."

"We'll find a way," Ella said, her forehead wrinkling. Genetic manipulation had solved so many problems, and finding another solution could take years, and by then, it might be too late. Our water supplies were actually coming from converted elemental energy of water elementals. "Maybe we can increase the amount of energy collectors."

"Yeah, and whose energy are they going to take if children are born with impure and weak elements? Or the disease? Then we better go look for an elixir of immortality, because otherwise... we're not going to stay here for long."

Ella's lips twisted into a wry smile. "No, we should find the mistake that turns these elementals into tainteds. They're not all tainteds, so that means there's been a mistake. Once that's fixed, there will be no more tainteds."

I threw myself on the bed, staring at the ceiling. Things might be easier if Jaiden and I turned ourselves in, but Sophia... she had to have a plan, and I wanted to know what it was.

My phone vibrated and I immediately grabbed it, checking the screen. It was a message from Nick. "Lily thinks there might be a way to retrieve some of the information about Sophia that was deleted and destroyed. She'll let us know once it's done, but she'll have to be careful because the media and the cops are all over her because they think she's helping us." I groaned.

"Let's hope she finds something."

"Yeah. If we make sure Sophia isn't a threat for every tainted elemental out there, then we can try to talk to the cops or give our side of the story." Actually, as long as I knew everyone else would be safe, I'd hand myself over to the cops. If they found me guilty for what I did and thought I needed to be punished, then so be it. I wouldn't be running from what I'd done for Elemontera or while I'd been under Blake's mind control.

Jaiden's hand found mine and I interlaced my fingers with his. "If she wants only us..." he started to say.

"...then she'll get us," I said. "But not anyone else. I'm not going to let innocent elementals pay for our mistakes."

Chapter 6

"Honey?" my mom's voice said quietly from the other end of the line.

"Mom?" I said with excitement. I'd been texting my parents whenever I could to let them know I was fine, but I didn't expect them to call me until it was perfectly safe.

"I need to see you," she said. "It's important."

"Sure. Where...?" My mom would never put my life at risk, so whatever she had to tell me definitely wasn't anything trivial.

"Two blocks away from your favorite bar. At the time you usually went to Magic Studies," she quickly said. "Stay safe."

She ended the call, and I met Jaiden's concerned eyes. "My mom wants to meet me in two hours."

"Why?" A frown appeared on Jaiden's brow. "Did something happen?"

"I guess. I don't know. She didn't want to say anything over the phone." The number she'd called from wasn't familiar, but that wasn't surprising. The cops were probably monitoring my parents to see if she'd contact me, so I hoped my mom had a good plan to avoid any unwanted tracers.

"Okay." Jaiden picked up a gun and tucked it into the back of his pants. I really hoped we wouldn't have to use any weapons or our elements.

I hovered above the place where my mom had told me to come, not willing to materialize until she came into view. Jaiden was crouching behind one of the cars, and I hoped the owner wouldn't appear anytime soon. Although, judging by the mud on and around the car, it hadn't been moved in a while. This alley was mostly abandoned, and there were high walls that remained after one of the buildings had been demolished. On the other side, there were two houses hidden behind thick trees, so it was unlikely someone would see us from one of the windows or a balcony.

Two figures in dark coats caught my attention, and as they approached, I recognized their faces. My mom's eyes darted from one corner to another, and I finally turned visible. Her shoulders slumping in relief, she rushed toward me and pulled me into a hug so tight I thought I wouldn't be able to breathe. My dad joined in, ruffling my hair.

"Thank God you're alright," my mom said, and when her face darkened, I knew Jaiden had come out from his hiding place. "Why is he here?"

"Mom..." We so didn't have time for my mom's disapproval of Jaiden.

"All of this is his fault," she hissed. "If he hadn't taken you to that God-awful Elemontera, you'd never have had to use those abilities..."

Jaiden paled slightly, and I glared at my mom. "Not now, Mom. Why did you want to see me?"

"Oh." She shook her head, patting her pocket for something, and then took out a flash drive. "This is all Lily could recover about Sophia."

"What did she find out?" I took the drive, too curious to wait to find out.

"I've no idea. We could barely transfer the data to the drive before the cops forced their way inside. They think she's helping you, so they're looking for any clues." She let out a heavy sigh. "But everything is here, so whatever it is... you'll have to find a way to use it. I'm not going to lose you because some crazy woman thinks you're..."

"You won't," I interrupted, clutching the drive in my hand and then placing it into a pocket on my jacket that had a zipper. If I lost the drive, I'd never forgive myself.

"Oh, sweetheart, come here." My mom pulled me into another hug, her eyes filling with tears, but when I withdrew, I could see her glaring at Jaiden over my shoulder.

"Mom, Dad, please stay safe," I said, but as I looked up at my dad, I spotted movement behind his back.

"Watch out!" I yelled, and tackled my dad to get him out of the way of a fireball. My mom ripped the silver element-blocking bracelet off her arm and faced the attacker. She had to have the bracelet on around my dad, who was a carrier and could feel her element, but now she needed her element.

But as I created a fireball, I noticed more elementals coming our way. There was at least a dozen of them and they were all ready to attack. Shit! I threw fireballs at the two closest to me, and then tried to blast another two with my air. Jaiden managed to push one of the attackers off his feet, and my mom was thrusting her air against another air elemental.

Who were these people? They were dressed completely in black, their faces covered with black masks. There were no symbols or anything on them, and I couldn't even tell if they were regular elementals or not. Dodging a waterball, I dropped to the ground and called to my air, guiding it out of me and toward one of the attackers.

But as I tried to slip my element inside his mind, my element bounced off some invisible force. What the hell? I increased the strength, just in case they were tainted elementals with an ability like mine that could sever my thread of energy, but no matter how hard I pushed, I couldn't break through. A gust of air hit me in the back, and my breath caught in my chest as I fell forward, a fireball nearly scorching my hand.

Creating a shield of air around me, I looked up at and saw Jaiden unsuccessfully trying to enter a person's mind. His shimmering thread went around the person's head, but then it just disappeared, as if he'd pulled it back, but I knew he hadn't. My mom was barely holding up her own shield in front of her and dad while the elements assaulted it. We were surrounded, and there was nowhere to go. Two more masked people appeared out of nowhere, but they didn't attack.

My shield was shimmering already, the water threatening to pierce right through it and get to me, but I gritted my teeth, increasing the strength and successfully shoving the water back until it disappeared. Enveloping my arms into fire, I was about to throw a fireball at the attackers when the assault of elements suddenly ceased and they all raised their hands up. What the hell?

Before I could react, they all unleashed their elements on us. I was thrown back, and when my vision cleared, I realized the only thing stopping the elements from hitting me was a thick layer of air.

Jaiden's brow was drawn in concentration, beads of sweat appearing on his forehead. My parents, he, and I were all huddled against the wall, his shield the only thing keeping us safe.

The elements crashed against the shield, trying to make an indent and break through it. As their power increased, Jaiden's hands started to shake and he clenched his jaw.

"Jaiden?" I asked. "We have to..."

"No, if I drop the shield, you won't have time to raise yours," he said. "Their elements are strong. I can feel them in every bone of my body. They'll break through. There's too many of them."

"What are we going to do?" I glanced at my parents, who were staring at the shield. Jaiden was right. We couldn't risk dropping it, but if we didn't do anything, his shield would give in eventually.

"Turn your parents into air," Jaiden said. "When the shield drops, fly like hell. You'll get them out. You're strong enough."

"What about you?" The elements were getting closer and closer. Jaiden's shield was thinning and he fell to his knees.

"Damn it, Moira, just go, okay? Don't worry about me. I'll fight them off somehow."

We didn't have much time, so I faced my parents. "Hold onto each other and take my hand." I hoped I could turn both of them into air even if they weren't directly touching me. Reaching out with my other hand toward Jaiden, I summoned my air. It was a surprise he could keep the shield up for so long under the assault of so many elements.

"Jaiden..."

"Now!" he yelled. His shield shimmered and burst outward, blasting the elements back toward the attackers. I immediately grabbed his hand and turned us all into air, darting toward the sky and not looking back.

My whole body felt heavy, my chest constricting. If I didn't land soon, I'd lose control of my element. Carrying three people after a fight wasn't an easy feat, and as soon as I was sure we were far enough, I descended on top of one building. Letting go of my parents and Jaiden, I scanned the sky for any shimmering, but I hoped the attackers had been knocked down by Jaiden's bursting shield long enough to leave me sufficient time to run away before they recovered. Since I couldn't see anything, I focused my attention back on my parents, who were getting to their feet, looking shaken but unharmed.

"That was..." My mom stumbled, running her hands up and down her body as if she was trying to check if all her body parts were still where they were supposed to be.

"What was that?" my dad asked, dusting off his pants.

"I've no idea." I said, my breathing still unsteady.

"Someone must have followed us." A vein throbbed in my mom's neck.

The problem was that we couldn't be sure if it had been someone who wanted to catch us for experiments, kill us, take us to Sophia, or maybe get a reward from the cops for turning us over. Great. But as I looked at Jaiden, I realized he was still lying on the ground and wasn't moving. I rushed to him and placed my hands on his face, my heart jumping into my throat, my blood racing. "Jaiden?"

His eyelids fluttered, but he didn't open his eyes. His skin was a bit cold to the touch and his hair was caked with sweat.

"Hey, can you hear me?" I asked, shaking him gently, but he only murmured something I couldn't understand. "No, Jaiden. Wake up."

"What's wrong with him?" My dad crouched next to us, a concerned expression on his face.

"His elements..." My voice cracked, because no, I didn't want to think that Jaiden might have drained his elements with that last attempt to stop the attackers. Keeping the shield up against so many elements and for so long must have taken a big amount of energy, but that didn't mean his elements were completely gone, and if they were... No. I pushed that thought away. He would be fine. He just needed some rest.

"What about them?" my dad asked.

"We need to find a safe place for him to recover." I let go of Jaiden and scrutinized the sky and our surroundings.

"He doesn't look well. Are you sure he doesn't need a doctor?"

"I..." I wasn't sure about anything because the only person who might know what would happen in case Jaiden completely drained his elements was his father, and he wasn't anywhere around for us to ask him.

My mom came closer, her gaze falling on Jaiden. "Do you think he drained his elements? It happened once to Ria and she fainted. Well, she was out for a while, but she's an element preserver and her elements weren't her own, so..."

Except that didn't mean a thing for Jaiden, because technically his elements weren't his own either, or maybe they were? Oh, God.

"We can take him to one of the old labs. No one will look for us there," my mom said, and I nodded. "Where is it?"

"Not far from here, but I don't know how we'll get there," she said.

I flexed my arms, and called to my air just enough to feel it surge through me. "I still have enough energy to carry all of you."

"Okay, then I'll show you..." She paused. "Wait, can I talk while we're... invisible?"

"Sure."

"Then I'll tell you."

I nodded, and placed my hand on Jaiden's chest. He'd be fine. He had to be.

Chapter 7

"Put him here," my mom said as she cleared off one of the beds. I fiddled with my air, trying to figure out how to turn Jaiden visible exactly where I wanted him. Focusing on the bed, I pushed what I thought was Jaiden above it, then slowly called my air back, revealing parts of his body. Finally visible, he was sprawled on the bed, his eyes closed, his face way too pale.

"Can you do anything?" I gave my mom a pleading look, then placed my hand on Jaiden's sweaty forehead. His breathing was shallow and his skin was still cold. Stepping back so my mom could come closer, I collided with a metal chair behind my back. The room was small, with light blue walls, and there were some devices covered with white blankets. My mom uncovered one of the devices that resembled a TV and pressed a button. The screen came to life, and various lines in different colors appeared across it.

"I'm not a doctor," my mom said, "but his vitals aren't looking too good. The levels of his elemental energy are almost nonexistent."

"Shit." I put my fist into my mouth and bit down. He had really drained his elements.

"I'm not sure if this is normal." A frown creased my mom's brow. "I know he used a lot of energy to keep that shield up, but someone with his power and abilities shouldn't have such low levels..." She looked up at me. "Has this ever happened to any tainted elemental? Or does this have something to do with his condition? Because of what you mentioned about him not being born with his elements?"

"I..." I took a deep breath. There was no point in keeping it a secret anymore. "Jaiden's elements aren't exactly permanent."

"What do you mean?" Her head jerked back.

"He has to take a serum so he can keep his elements."

"A serum?" She let go of Jaiden's arm and came toward me. "What kind of serum? Does that mean anyone could get a second element if they took...?"

"No, the serum works only on Jaiden. His father is the only one who knows how to make it, and if Jaiden doesn't take it... I guess his elements start to fade when he uses them a lot. And since his father is on the run... Jaiden hasn't taken the serum. He gave it to me so I could go after Blake."

She tilted her head. "You gave me something to analyze to try and recreate... Was that...?" She narrowed her eyes at me.

"Yeah. It was the serum, but you said you couldn't do it, so..." The beginning of a headache was starting to form behind my eyes.

"It was unique. I've never seen anything like it." She glanced at Jaiden over her shoulder. "So what happens to him if he doesn't take the serum? Will he lose his second element? Or both?"

"I don't know. I don't think he's ever gone so long without the serum when his elemental energy was low. I don't even know what can happen." Jaiden looked so weak and barely alive. If he was losing one or both of his elements, wouldn't he at least be conscious?

"I only have experience with element preservers and regular elementals, but losing elements can cause this kind of reaction... but his case is different because his element or maybe both were affected by whatever his father did to him." For the first time, my mom's eyes softened as she looked back at Jaiden.

I ran my hand across my face and let out a loud sigh. "Is there anything you can do or anyone you could call for help?"

My mom shook her head. "I'd call Lily, but she can't send any help right now when everyone's watching her, and the others... I doubt they have experience with tainted elementals or would even want to help someone who is a murder suspect."

"Right." I couldn't just sit here and wait. As I lowered my hand, my fingers brushed against the pocket with the flash drive. "Is there a computer somewhere in here?"

"Yeah, just down the hallway."

"I'm going to see what's on this." I took out the drive and waved with it. "If something changes or if he wakes up, let me know immediately."

My mom nodded. "Go. I'll take care of him."

"Thanks." I offered her a weak smile and headed out. The hallway was empty, its gray floor slightly slippery, but not even its light blue walls could calm me. When I reached the door at the end, I peeked inside and saw my father sitting on one of the sofas. The old-looking computer was on the table, half covered with a blue blanket.

"How is he?" my dad asked, the lines around his blue eyes more prominent.

"I don't know." My voice was shaky and my dad got to his feet and came toward me, placing his arms around me. I fought the urge to burst into tears as he ran circles across my back.

"Oh, honey, he'll be fine. You'll see," he said.

I only nodded, then squeezed the drive in my hand and pulled away. "We need to see what's on this." We had all risked way too much to get the damn thing. There better be something useful on it.

I started the computer, and a soft fuzzy noise came out of it. Pulling a nearby chair closer, I took a seat in front of the screen and waited at least five minutes for the damn thing to start. After sliding the drive into the slot, I put my hand over the mouse and clicked multiple times to get the files to open.

There didn't seem to be much information, and one file contained Lily's apology for not being able to recover much because whoever Sophia had hired had done one hell of a good job. My dad leaned over my shoulder, squinting at the screen.

"Looks like Sophia is her real name, or at least she had it legally changed at some point," I said in surprise. "She's twenty-six, came to town for college, and one day just stopped going to classes. Huh."

There was no information about where she could've come from or what she'd been studying, but it was a start. We could track her down in the college's records. Hopefully. I scrolled down and saw Sophia's name was in Elemontera's system, but there was no way to recover the files that would explain why she was mentioned. Great, so Jaiden's father had something to do with it and our theory that Sophia was working with him could be right.

"Wait, we went through all that trouble to get this?" My dad scowled at the screen, taking the mouse from me and trying to scroll farther, but there was nothing except blank pages. "Seriously, Lily? That was all you got?"

"It's enough, actually." I pushed myself to my feet. "There has to be something about her in the records that couldn't be deleted. And now we know how old she is, so narrowing it down won't be so hard." At least I hoped it wouldn't. Surely we'd have heard if someone had broken into the college's building and stolen some papers.

"I'm surprised no one recognized her. If she went to college..."

"Maybe she looked different, or she wasn't one of the memorable faces and didn't hang out with people. The college is full of students, so it's impossible to know everyone. Maybe some of them are working for her or she found another way to ensure they keep their mouths shut." I disconnected the flash drive and put it back into my pocket. It wasn't much information, but I didn't want to leave it here for just anyone to find.

"So you're going to dig through a bunch of papers at the college and hope you find out more about her?" He pursed his lips.

"No, I'm going to send someone to take care of that." I was already getting a hold of my phone so I could text Noah.

"Smart. Giving boring tasks to your buddies." A slow grin spread across my father's lips, then his face became serious again. "Wait, then what are you going to do? Stay here with Jaiden?"

"No, I'm going to find his father."

"What?" He gaped at me. "How? Why?"

"I don't know yet how, but I have plenty of reasons to find him. He has something that can help Jaiden, and Sophia was in Elemontera's system, so Jack has to know her." There was no way she was in the system without his knowledge. I wanted to know what her role was. She was too old to be a tainted elemental, but she could have been a researcher or a regular agent.

"If you say so... but Jack has been on the run for a while. It won't be easy to track him down."

I chewed on the insides of my cheek, aware that my father was right.

"Honey!" My mom's voice pierced the air. I turned into air without thinking and flashed myself right next to her. She gasped, flinching back, but then she relaxed when I fully materialized. Jaiden's eyes cracked open, and he was moving his arms. I nearly fell over from relief.

"Jaiden? Are you okay?" I rushed to his side, taking his shaky hand into mine and placing a soft kiss on his knuckles.

"Hey." He flashed me a weak smile. "Is everyone safe?"

"Yeah, we managed to get away." I sat on the edge of the bed. "How are you feeling?"

"Terrible." He grimaced. "But it doesn't matter. You're okay."

"I'll be right outside," my mom said, inclining her head toward us, and scooted out of the room. As the door closed, Jaiden coughed.

"I checked the files about Sophia. There isn't much, but she's somehow connected to Elemontera. We just don't know how," I said.

"Figures." He pressed his lips into a tight line. "Who else would be behind everything if not my father?"

"I'm going after him."

Jaiden's head snapped toward me, his eyes widening. "No, you're not."

"Yes, I am. You need the serum and we need the info he has about Sophia."

"No. I won't let you go." He lifted his chin, his gaze alert. "So what if Sophia was in Elemontera's system? She wasn't anyone important or I'd know about her. Anything he could tell you won't matter. We need to figure out her next move and act before she ruins everything."

"I know, but you're not in the condition to..."

"I told you not to worry about me." He gave me a hard look. "I meant it. No matter what happens to me, don't go after my father."

"But if he's helping her... or if they're working together... then by finding him, I might find her. Believe me, that's the best shot we've got."

"By now he could've reorganized the men who used to work for him. He might have too many people protecting him, and if they catch you... You don't know him like I do. If he wants to rebuild Elemontera, he'll be ruthless."

"All we know is that he took that recovery file for Elemontera, but that doesn't mean he could've reorganized already. I'll be careful. I promise."

"Moira, no!" He raised his voice, trying to push himself up, but he fell back against the pillows.

"I'm going to get that serum for you."

"How many times do I have to tell you no? I don't want it, okay? I don't want anything from my father anymore. We'll figure this out. I can live without my elements... I can..." He blinked, licking his dry and cracked lips. He wasn't getting any better. I didn't need to be a doctor to notice that. He was trying to be strong for me because he thought he could protect me, but I wasn't about to change my mind.

"It's my choice. Please," he finally said, his eyes boring into mine.

I averted my gaze, biting down on my lower lip. When I looked up at him, my voice was steady and calm. "And it's my choice to go after your father."

"Fine." He clenched his jaw, resting his head on the pillows and staring at the wall. "But I won't help you find him."

"Okay." I swallowed hard. My phone vibrated and I realized it was Noah texting me back, promising he was going to check the college's records. I leaned forward and brushed my lips against Jaiden's, then turned myself into air, ready to find his father no matter what. Jack Maiers was somewhere out there and I would do anything to get him.

Chapter 8

When I returned to the lab some ten hours later, I nearly fell off my feet from exhaustion. After a quick check-up on Jaiden and finding him asleep, I tiptoed out of the room and went down the hallway. My parents were seated around the computer, their faces grim.

"What's wrong?" I asked, and they both jumped.

"Oh God, honey, I didn't know you were back," my mom said. As she moved her head, I could see two small windows on the screen. On one, I recognized Noah's face.

"Moira, are you there?" He waved his hand. "I can hear you, but that stupid computer of yours doesn't have a camera so I can't see you."

"Yeah, I'm here," I said, coming closer. "Did you find anything?"

"Well, sort of." His face fell, then he bobbed his head to the left. "Oh wait, I'm not sure if the other window is on the right or left. Shit. Just look at it."

I focused on the video that was playing next to Noah's. A group of people in black were blasted back by a shield of air... "Someone filmed the attack on us?" I looked at my mom and dad.

"Sophia's men did," she said, her face sour.

"You're not going to like this," Noah said.

"What did she do now? Accuse us of attacking her people even though they attacked first?" I clenched my jaw.

"Not exactly. She broadcast another video in which she's taking full responsibility of the attack on Jaiden and you."

"Why would she do that?"

"Just watch," Noah said, and my mom restarted the video. Sophia's face flashed across the screen for a moment, and then the video of Jaiden and me meeting with my parents came up.

"The cops are having trouble locating and hunting down these two murderers," Sophia said. "But it seems like they're not trying hard enough. Our government isn't competent enough to deal with this. As you can see, my small team of untrained elements almost captured the fugitives. If we all work together, we'll get them."

I swore under my breath. So that was what Sophia had been planning: to capture Jaiden and me and take all the credit for it, maybe even get people's support because of it. Wonderful.

"I've heard some of you out there sympathize with these people, but let me tell you something. If they were good people, they'd turn over those two criminals and not protect them. Good people of this city, come to the square and let's show the government and those elementals that we're not afraid and that together we can handle this. The nightmares that haunt this city can be defeated! Moira and Jaiden, I'm talking to you now. If you want to show everyone that your kind is not as bloodthirsty as they seem, come to the main square in five hours and turn yourselves in. We want to hear your side of the story, too. We're not monsters." The screen went black.

"Perfect. Just fucking perfect." I didn't know if Sophia would truly appear at the square, but I was sure she'd come accompanied by her men, who wouldn't let anything happen to her. Hell, the angry mob that would come out just to see her or to complain about something would be there to protect her too. "If Jaiden and I don't appear there, she'll say we're hiding because we have reasons to do it, and I'm sure some people will agree with her."

"You're not actually considering going there," Noah said.

"No, it's a trap. She wants to provoke us and get us to attack her, and if we do that, people won't care that she started it first. Whatever we do, she wins." I gritted my teeth. "I don't like this at all."

"Yeah, me neither. So what are we going to do? If she really appears, it's an opportunity to track her down and try to capture her, but I'm sure she'll take all the necessary precautions," Noah said.

"I doubt she'll let anyone near her. Those people who attacked us will make sure of it, if she doesn't have more elsewhere. No, we definitely can't make a move, but we can monitor her." I scratched my chin.

Noah cocked his head to the side. "Monitor her how?"

"Send Marissa, Sam, and Ashley to the square to join the people and see what Sophia says. Make sure they don't reveal themselves as tainteds to anyone."

"What?" Noah gasped. "Are you crazy? I can't send them into an angry crowd!"

"It's unlikely someone will recognize them if they don't use their elements. Tell them to change their appearance a bit just in case." Sophia wouldn't attack random people because she suspected they were elementals. No, she had to have a bigger plan. She wanted us to attack first or make it seem like we did so she could blame all of us for being evil and bloodthirsty.

"No, I'll go myself," Noah said. "Maybe take Nick with me."

"You can't. You were both in Elemontera's system as their agents, and if Sophia is really working with Jaiden's father, then she probably has access to that file. She and her men could be looking for familiar faces from

Elemontera or have some other means of detecting Elemontera's ex agents. You mustn't go there."

"Shit." Noah chewed on his lower lip. "What do you think her end game is? She's mostly focusing on Jaiden and you."

"I wish I knew. Maybe she's planning to run for mayor." She was really trying to make it look like she cared about the city and its people. That didn't sound very different from political campaigns.

"Couldn't she have just bribed someone for that when she has so many connections?"

"Probably, but that wouldn't be real enough for her, I guess. Hopefully Jaiden's father will tell me more."

"You don't know where he is, do you?"

"No, I've been looking all over for him, but no luck." I studied Noah's face. "Did my mom tell you Jaiden might be dying?"

"What?" Noah's composure broke for a moment, but he quickly masked it.

"He's losing his elements. They're not like ours. His father did something to him so he'd have them, but he needs a serum to keep them or else... I don't know."

"Losing his elements? But why would he die because of that?" Noah's brow furrowed, and I knew he still cared about Jaiden, even though he was still hurt by Jaiden's betrayal.

"Maybe he won't, but... if you want to come talk to him... you might want to do it soon." I had absolutely no intention of letting Jaiden die, but if he and Noah could patch things up or at least if Noah could let go of his anger at Jaiden a little bit... it might be a good thing for them both.

"Okay." He nodded gravely. "Talk to you later."

I inclined my head and the window went black.

"I'm going to check up on Jaiden," I said to my parents and started down the hallway. When I entered his room, his eyes were still closed, so I settled at the edge of the bed and bent down to place a feather-like kiss on his cheek. His eyelids fluttered and he looked up at me.

"Hey," I said, my lips spreading into a smile.

"Hey," he rasped, smiling back.

"Feeling any better?" I asked, although he didn't really look like it. His face was still deathly pale, his skin clammy and cold.

"Not really."

"Listen, I know you don't want me to go after your father, but we have no choice. He could be the key to getting you better and solving our Sophia problem. Do you know any places where your father could go to hide?"

"No." Jaiden's eyes flashed with intensity. "I won't tell you anything."

"Why not? Even if you don't want anything from him anymore, that doesn't mean we have to risk the lives of every tainted elemental because we didn't dare talk to him about Sophia. Please." I ran my hand down his cheek.

"No." A frown line appeared on his forehead, and he blinked at me.

"I think it's the only way to stop Sophia. She has another plan to lure us out in the open and make a spectacle of us or whatever. We can't let her do this to us and other tainteds," I pleaded.

"I can't..." He narrowed his eyes, his hands starting to shake slightly.

"I don't understand. If you only get weaker and we don't find a way to stop Sophia or thwart her plans, what then? I thought you wanted to help those like us."

"I won't tell you anything." He raised his arm and placed it over his head.

"Yeah, you keep repeating that." I bit the inside of my lip. "But you're not giving me any good explanations, so... if you have a really good reason except that you're afraid that your father might have protection and that I could get caught, then tell me. Otherwise..."

"I..." Jaiden coughed, then shook his head. "Something... something's wrong."

"What?" I put my hands on both sides of his face and met his dark eyes. "What's wrong?"

"I can't tell you anything." He bit down on his lip so hard he drew blood. "Why can't I...?"

"Shit." I let go of him. "Do you think someone mind-controlled you?"

He only gave me a brief nod, his eyes wide. Well, that was a problem. "But how? When?" I raised my finger before he could try to say anything because I was sure he couldn't tell me what he wanted to. "I can help you." Calling to my air, I guided a thin thread toward Jaiden's head and tried to gently push inside, but my air slammed into a barrier.

"Can you let me in? I can fix this." I'd healed other elementals' minds before, including my own, so I believed that I could do the same with Jaiden if I could get inside his mind and see the blackened brain signals. But as I pushed a bit stronger with my air, the barrier still stayed, and Jaiden winced, so I pulled back.

"Do it," he panted. "Just do it."

I focused on my element again, making the shimmering thread dance around Jaiden's head and using more force to get it inside, but the barrier was still there, and this time he cried out. My stomach did a nervous flip and I took a deep breath. There was no other way to do this because Jaiden didn't know how to heal his own brain signals, and even if he did, I doubted he'd have the energy for it. I might have done it once and risked my own sanity in the process, but I'd been strong enough.

"It's okay." He gripped my arm. "Don't be afraid. Do it."

I closed my eyes, blocking every thought out of my mind. If I wanted to do this, I had to ignore Jaiden's pain, and that was much harder than anything else. I wasn't sure if it hurt more because he was weak right now or because he'd been mind-controlled to protect his own mind, no matter what. Something told me it was the latter.

I gathered my strength and shoved my air into Jaiden's head, pushing and pushing until I finally slipped through. A scream pierced the air, but all I could see were the darkened signals in front of me. There weren't many, which was probably the reason Jaiden hadn't realized something was wrong, but someone had done a good job, and it had been someone powerful enough to break through Jaiden's protection. I hoped we wouldn't be dealing with another Blake.

I forced my element into the signals, capturing them and feeding them back until they were restored to their white color, or at least that was what I pictured in my mind.

As soon as I was done, I let my element slam back into me and opened my eyes, almost dreading what I might see. The tension sipped out of my shoulders when Jaiden looked at me.

"Are you okay?" I asked.

"Yeah." His nostrils flared. "I can't believe someone mind-controlled me not to look for my father."

"Do you know who it was?" I leaned forward.

He shook his head. "Whoever it was, they were standing behind me... in that hallway that led to that room where I'd been keeping my father." He narrowed his eyes. "My father didn't escape because someone helped him. It was me. I left the door open and then later came back to close it." He gritted his teeth, trying to push himself up, but I placed my hand on his chest.

"Don't waste your strength. Is there anything else you remember about that person?"

"The voice... it was male," he said. "He ordered me to free my father, forget about it, and to stop looking for him."

I rubbed my forehead. Great, another strong elemental who was working against us, but why? Why would anyone help Jaiden's father and want to make sure Jaiden didn't know he'd let his father out? Someone who was clearly trying to hide his existence. One more reason to find Jack as soon as possible. I just hoped the elemental wasn't someone who wanted Jack dead. "Do you know what that person could want with your father?"

"No clue. If it was to keep me away so I couldn't protect him..." Jaiden frowned. "If he's dead, then..."

"Okay, let's not jump to conclusions. Your father is a resourceful man. Maybe the elemental was working for him. Going through so much trouble just to kill him seems strange."

"Yeah, you're right." He looked around. "Do you have a phone or a map? I know the places my father used to frequent and maybe somewhere he would seek shelter or just pass by..."

"Sure." I fished my phone out of my pocket and handed it to him, praying that Jack was still alive, which had to be the weirdest thing ever. But the information and the serum he had were very valuable to both Jaiden and me.

Chapter 9

I groaned as I crossed out yet another spot on the map that Jaiden had indicated. His father was nowhere to be seen, and I was already starting to lose hope that I'd find him or that he was even still alive. But as I flew between the cars in the parking lot in front of a club Jack apparently loved to visit, I spotted a black car with tinted windows.

Circling the car, I found the ventilation system and slipped through it, squeezing my shimmering cloud. As I popped out into the car, I landed on the back seat and noticed a phone just lying there on the seat with a piece of paper tucked underneath it. Turning myself visible, I carefully picked up the phone and inspected the note. My heart skipped a beat when I saw my name written across it in a neat handwriting.

Sliding my finger across the screen of the phone, I brought it to life and found only one number in the contacts. There wasn't anything else on the phone. Obviously, it was meant for me. Someone had known I'd come here, which made me uneasy. What if this was one of

Sophia's sick games? Did she have anything to do with Jaiden's mind-controlling and Jack's release? But why would she work with tainteds if she hated them so much?

I lifted the phone and checked the battery, just to make sure it wasn't a bomb that would detonate when I made the call. The phone seemed clean, so I turned it into air and left the car. I didn't want any hidden attackers to jump on me if whoever had left the phone expected me to stay trapped in the car.

When I found a spot safe enough, I tapped my finger against the number and pressed the phone to my ear. Something clicked on the other end of the line, but no one answered. I waited for a moment, and a soft noise could be heard in the background.

"Mr. Maiers?" I asked, scanning my surroundings just in case someone was tracking the phone.

"I'm glad you called," Jack said, and the happy sound in his voice made me sure that he wasn't being held captive anywhere. Well, unless he'd been mind-controlled.

"Is that so?" I said, wondering how much he knew about what was going on.

"I've been expecting you. Is my son with you?"

"Why?" I didn't want to tell him anything just yet.

"You know why. I saw that video on the news. Jaiden's elements couldn't have withstood that. How is he?" I could swear I'd heard worry tint Jack's voice. Was he really concerned about Jaiden?

"Not well. He needs the serum."

"Yes, he does. Bring him to me and we'll fix him."

Fix him? Great. "No, you'll give me the serum and I'll take it to Jaiden."

"That's not how things will go. You'll bring him to me and your friends won't follow. Understood?"

"No." It was impressive how he expected me to just bend to his will. "What do you want with Jaiden? Give me the serum and that's it. You owe him that after all you've done."

"Now, now, Moira," Jack said dryly. "You're forgetting one thing. If Jaiden doesn't get the serum soon, he'll die."

There wasn't anything in Jack's voice to indicate that he was lying and I bit the inside of my cheek. My fears had been right. I needed that serum, but if Jack wanted us to come to him, that meant he had other plans. Plans that would undoubtedly benefit him and prove to be a problem for us.

"You won't let him die," I said.

"Ah, but neither will you," he said. "Agree to my terms or we'll both have to live with the consequences of your decision."

My eyebrows shot up. My decision? Yeah, Jack would lay the blame on me with no problem. Fuck. "Okay. I'll bring him to you."

"Good. Keep the phone. I'll send you a message," he said. "And don't even try to trace the call. You won't catch me. And if anyone comes with you or follows you, I'll have to disappear, and that'll lower Jaiden's chances of survival. Please make sure my son stays alive in the meantime."

I had to fight the urge to chuck the phone at the wall across the street. "Did you have someone mind-control him to let you out? Was it Sophia?"

"See you soon." The line went dead, and I clenched my fingers around the phone. Jack was hiding something, and oh yeah, he at least knew who Sophia was. The only problem was how to get the information and Jaiden's serum without ending up in Jack's clutches.

I didn't trust Jaiden's father at all, and I knew I'd have to be extra careful. But Jaiden needed the serum and I wouldn't let him die, even if Jack found a way to capture me. We had no other choice as long as Jack was the only one with the formula for the serum. Maybe it was time to change that, but I'd have to figure out a way to force the information out of him or steal it somehow. My mom hadn't been able to recreate it before, but if she knew exactly what had to be done, step by step, then maybe she'd have a better chance.

Chapter 10

When I got back to the lab, I almost ran into Noah. "Hey," I said, a smile tugging at my lips.

Noah's lips quirked up briefly, but he looked tired and worried. "Did you find his father?"

"Yeah, kind of. I spoke to him." I started toward Jaiden's room and leaned at the doorway. Jaiden's eyes were closed, his chest barely moving up and down. "He wants me to bring Jaiden to him."

"What? Why?" Noah gaped at me.

"He doesn't want to hand over the serum, and probably has some twisted plan in mind, as usual." I stretched my arms, my muscles aching.

"But you can't just take Jaiden to him! If he's working with Sophia... and even if he's not, it's still too dangerous to trust him. Why wouldn't he just name his price and give you the serum?"

"I don't know. He didn't say much, just that it would be my fault if I didn't get Jaiden to him in time, or refused to bring him." I banged my head lightly against the doorway.

"So he could really... die?" Noah's eyes were filled with worry.

"Yeah." I stared at my feet. "I can't let that happen."

"I know... I just..." He glanced at Jaiden, then back at me. "Isn't there another way to...?"

I shook my head. "I wish there was, but not yet, and we don't have time to do experiments."

"What are we going to do then?" Noah asked. "You can't just go there alone. Maiers might want to capture or hurt you."

"We have no choice. He would run if he saw someone coming with me, and then it might be too late for Jaiden. I won't take that risk."

"So you're just going to do as he says?" Noah raised his voice.

"Yeah." I gave him a long look and noticed my mom coming toward us.

"What's going on? Did you find the serum?" my mom asked as she stopped next to Noah.

"Jack wants me to bring Jaiden to him." I raised my finger before she could say anything. "I've made my choice. This is the only chance Jaiden has, so I'll take him wherever Jack wants."

"Are you sure that's a good idea? Jack might be lying to lure you out," my mom said. "He's not an honorable man. If he cared about his son, he would've already sent him the serum or would have given it to you."

"I'm well aware of the danger," I said.

"What if Jaiden won't die? What if he's just feeling sick until the elements completely vanish from his body?" Noah asked.

"Do you think we should just wait and see?" I met Noah's eyes.

He licked his lips, his gaze flying to Jaiden. "No," he finally said, sighing. "We can't do that."

"Can we send someone else with Jaiden?" my mom asked. "You don't have to go. You're too valuable to Jack because of your abilities."

"It has to be me. I doubt Jack would agree to anyone else coming, and besides, my abilities give me a better chance of confronting him." Risking someone else's life wouldn't be a good idea, and if Jack actually wanted Jaiden and not me, he'd have to let me live if he wanted Jaiden to cooperate. Losing me wouldn't make Jaiden the most agreeable person in the world.

My mom's eyes filled with tears, but she pushed them back. "I know, but..." She stepped forward and wrapped her arms tightly around me. "I wish there was something else we could do."

"Me too." I looked over her shoulder at Noah. "Did you come here because you have news on Sophia or...?"

"No." Noah scratched his head. "I came to see Jaiden. We spoke... and I... He was glad to see me."

I let go of my mom and gave him a brief nod. The phone Jack left for me vibrated, and I immediately checked it. "Jack just texted me the address. I have to go."

"Where does he want to meet you?" Noah asked, his eyes alert.

"Downtown. Public place."

"Do you want me to go with you? I'd stay out of sight."

"No. No way. I don't want Jack to get scared and run." I turned to my mom. "Is there some kind of a device that could alert you of my location or something?"

"I'll go look around for it." My mom rushed down the hallway.

"Be careful," Noah said.

"I will." I headed into Jaiden's room, hoping Jack wouldn't try to trick me, because if he did, I would be really, really pissed off.

Chapter 11

Jack was standing in front of a car with tinted windows, his hands in the pockets of his black coat. As I flew closer, he took something out of his pocket and looked at it, a slow smile spreading across his lips. As if he knew I was there, he opened the door of the car and I flew inside, settling into the back seat. Materializing Jaiden and myself, I looked up at Jack.

"Hello, Moira," he said, closing the door and then getting into the driver's seat.

"How did you know I was here?" No one except those like us could see the shimmering, so I suspected the device had something to do with it. I just didn't know what it was.

"Energy levels detector," he said, starting the car. "Very useful thing."

"Weren't you afraid someone might see you out here in the open? You're still a fugitive." The cops had to be looking for Jack too, since he was responsible for everything that had happened in Elemontera, but because

Jaiden had saved him, no one had been able to locate him, or Jack had connections that had allowed him to escape.

"Not really." He glanced at me in the rearview mirror. "Haven't seen any cops around here and not many people can recognize me."

"Where are we going?" I asked, watching the people in the street. Jaiden let out a soft moan, his head resting in my lap, and I placed my hand on his cheek.

"You'll see." Jack turned in his seat to look at Jaiden, and I thought I was hallucinating the concerned expression on his face.

"Will Sophia be there too?" I checked around the car for any strange devices that could be used to trap me, but I didn't see anything. Still, I had to be very careful, especially if there was an elemental who could mind-control me. "Or that tainted elemental who helped you escape?"

"You're asking all the wrong questions." Jack turned on the music and upped the volume. "We'll talk once we get to the lab."

The lab? So Jack already had a lab, or maybe it was one of his old ones that no one knew about. I didn't like the sound of that. The car swerved into an abandoned alley and sped toward the old factory at the end. My mouth went dry when I realized Jack wasn't slowing down, and we were rapidly approaching the building's dark red rusty metal wall.

Before I could say anything, the wall parted and we passed through. We reached another set of doors that lifted and revealed a long, dark tunnel. At the end of it was a parking lot with a few cars, and a big glass door with elemental protection, similar to what Jack had had in Elemontera. Shit. This was probably a trap. If he could've kept us in Elemontera, he could keep us here too. The car pulled up into one of the free spots.

"Can you carry him inside?" Jack opened the door and got out of the car.

"Why don't you get one of your men to do that?" I cocked my head at him, pushing at the door.

"I would, but they're not here."

Wonderful. He wanted me inside, and there wasn't really anything I could do about it. Besides, I wasn't about to leave Jaiden alone with his father. Biting down on my lip, I turned Jaiden and myself into air and hovered in front of the entrance.

"Follow me." Jack started toward the door and pressed his hand against the keypad. After a whole set of protective measures, he stepped back and the door opened. I flew inside and nearly crashed into a wall. Everything seemed so much like Elemontera... metal walls, no windows, pristinely clean floor... No, this wasn't Elemontera, even if Jack was planning to rebuild it in this place.

"In here." Jack nodded toward an open door and we ended up in what looked like a real lab, complete with tables, instruments, computers, and shelves full of various liquids. One of the tables was big enough for a person to lie down on, so I directed Jaiden's shimmering cloud toward it. Or was that *my* cloud since I was the one turning him into air? Oh God. We both materialized, and Jaiden pried his eyes open.

"Moira..." he whispered, but then his eyes closed again, and I grabbed his hand.

"Jaiden? I'm here." I looked at Jack, who was putting on a pair of white latex gloves and busying himself with something. "Hurry! He's not..."

"He'll be fine." Jack turned his back to me. "You can leave if you want. You brought my son to me and that's all I wanted."

"No, I'll stay."

"Suit yourself." Jack approached the table, his gaze falling on Jaiden. He picked up a knife and I stepped in front of him.

"What are you doing with that?"

"Relax. I need to cut his shirt open. Now get out of my way before it's too late. And don't bother me again," he said coldly.

Crossing my arms, I stepped away and took a seat in one of the chairs, not close enough to get in Jack's way, but not too far either so I could jump at him if he made a wrong move. Jack ripped Jaiden's shirt with the help of the knife and placed some kind of a rectangular, bluish metallic device on Jaiden's chest.

Something started to beep, and I noticed that one of the screens at the end of the room had come to life and was showing Jaiden's vitals, which were dangerously low. His elements were almost nonexistent, just a tiny dot of light. There was some data and stats I didn't even understand, but I thought they had to do something with Jaiden's DNA.

Jack dashed across the room and picked up a syringe. "Stay with me, Jaiden. Come on."

But as he brought the syringe toward Jaiden's neck, I noticed the liquid in it wasn't its usual color; this one was silver. I jumped to my feet in an instant.

"What are you giving him?" I yelled, but before I could reach him, Jack already released the liquid into Jaiden's system.

I let out a blast of air and sent Jack flying. His back hit the wall, his breath leaving his chest in a whoosh, and I pinned him with my element. Stalking toward him, I narrowed my eyes.

"What was in that syringe? Tell me!"

"The serum he needs to survive." He glared at me. "What do you think you're doing?"

"That's not the serum. I've seen it!"

A loud beeping sound pierced the air, and I turned my attention to the computer, letting go of Jack, who slumped to the ground. Jaiden's elemental energy seemed to be increasing really fast, so I ran toward the table.

"Jaiden?"

His eyes flew open, a gasp escaping his lips. "Moira?" He sat up, looking around in confusion. Then his whole body started to shake, and I had to catch him so he wouldn't fall. His arms went invisible, and the shimmering spread until he was completely turned into air. His cloud rose up into the air and whizzed past me and toward Jack.

"What did you do to me?" Jaiden yelled.

Jack leaned against the wall, the corners of his lips tilting up. "Saved you, son. I saved you."

Chapter 12

Jaiden materialized right in front of his father. "Give me one good reason why I shouldn't kill you right here and now."

"Ah, but if I die, you won't find out anything about Sophia and won't get another dose of the improved serum I just gave you." Jack looked as smug as the cat who just ate the canary.

"Improved serum? What's it going to do?" I asked, coming to stand next to Jaiden.

"Give him permanent elements," Jack said proudly.

"What?" Jaiden gaped at him.

"You need five more doses of this stronger serum and your elements should be permanent."

"Should be?" I raised my voice. "Don't tell me you just experimented on..."

"Yes, yes." He gave me a deadpan look. "It isn't as if I could test this on rats or anyone else. We'll see if it works, but it should." He faced Jaiden. "You can feel it inside of you, can't you?"

"It's like my elements are... bigger than they used to be." Jaiden frowned. "I don't..."

"Don't worry. The feeling should wear off as you get used to it."

"Where are the rest of the doses?" I asked, my hands curling into fists.

"Oh, as if I'm going to tell you that." Jack grinned, and Jaiden's air slammed into him so hard that he coughed.

"You'll tell us everything." Jaiden's air went toward Jack's head, but it bounced off.

"Oh please. Just because your elements are little bit stronger now doesn't mean you can get past my protection." Jack tapped the back of his head.

Calling to my own air, I pushed with all my strength toward Jack's mind, but my air was stopped by the barrier too. How the hell was he doing that? He couldn't have protection against me, or could he?

"Now, now Moira. I managed to replicate your elemental energy and enhance it, then tweak the device to block you out too, and any other elementals."

Jaiden swore, running a hand through his hair. I was glad the color was returning to his face, but I wasn't sure about the new serum.

"Why did you do it?" Jaiden finally asked, his eyes desperate. "Why did you give me that serum? Just to see how it would work out or because you want me to do something for you?"

"I wanted you to live," Jack said. "But yeah, there's one little thing I want you to take care of for me, and then I'll give you another dose of the serum."

"Is it a kill job?" Jaiden pressed his lips into a tight line.

"Perhaps." Jack's lips twisted into a cruel smile. "But you'll be glad when I tell you who the target is."

"Really?" I ground my teeth together. "You're going to ask for something in return? Wow. Just wow."

"It's Sophia Mornell," Jack said. "Or whatever she calls herself these days. I want you to catch her and get her out of my way."

"Why?" I asked. "What do you know about her?"

"She's after me, and I'm not really inclined to part with this life just yet." Jack's face grew serious.

"Why is she after you? We know she was in Elementera's system. Who is she?" I asked.

"Her name used to be Anne Harnett," Jack said. "She was one of my experiments."

"Your experiments? How?" I wasn't surprised that Sophia used to have another name, but she must have taken the new name a long time ago or else there wouldn't be any records of her... unless, she planted them there for us to find. But why would she do that? To make it harder for us to track her down? Perhaps.

"She was very interested in tainted elementals and wanted to be one of them, so I granted her wish."

"You couldn't have," Jaiden said. "All your experiments on adults were failures. They all died within a week or so."

"Well, yes, that's what we all thought." Jack's face turned sour.

"What do you mean?" I searched his eyes. "Are you telling us Sophia is one of us?"

"Yeah, that's exactly what I'm telling you." He grimaced. "I gave her a testing batch of my new, improved serum to turn adults into tainted elementals, but... she was dead in two days. I checked her vitals and I was sure she was dead, just like another experiment... but somehow both she and Terry came back to life."

"What?" I gaped at him. "But how?"

"I don't know. I assume the body couldn't withstand the elements, but instead of dying completely, the elements flared back up after a day or two, and the energy was enough to revive the body. She came to me, and I did some tests, but I couldn't determine what exactly happened. Maybe she didn't die at all, but it seemed so because her elemental energy confused our detectors that were unable to check her vitals properly." Jack sighed. "It doesn't really matter. I tried it again with others, but it didn't work."

"When did that happen?" Jaiden asked, tipping his head to the side.

"While you were hiding on Roivenna." Jack gave his son such a judging look that I wanted to punch him. "I tried to train her in utmost secrecy, but when she saw the extent of tainteds' abilities... she found an opportunity to run away. I haven't seen or heard about her until she appeared on the TV, and then sent me a threatening message. I've been looking for her everywhere, but without luck. I don't think she can be controlled, so it's better if we get rid of her."

"She threatened you?" I asked. "How?"

"She said she'd take everything from me and make sure I never help create another killer."

"What kind of abilities does she have? What are her elements?" Jaiden asked.

"Air and earth," Jack said. "While I was training her, she could only turn into air, but she might be able to control minds and kill too."

"Great." I threw my hands up in despair. We weren't just dealing with a person who didn't like tainted elementals. We were against one of our own... one who might be able to control the minds of who knows how many people and come after us. Oh God.

"What about the other person?" Jaiden met his father's gaze.

"He's unstable..." Jack shook his head. "Terry Garrly, an air and water elemental. He disappeared with Sophia, but he might have been more affected by his transformation. My men have spotted him in the city, but weren't able to catch him. He didn't cause me trouble or resurface after that, so he might be dead or gone by now."

"Why didn't you just tell me any of this?" Jaiden groaned. "I could've found them before this shit happened."

"I intended to, actually," Jack said. "But for some reason I didn't..."

"Terry mind-controlled you, didn't he? Or Sophia? Are you sure your men really saw him or do you just think they did?" I doubted Jack had set up his protection so fast, because he didn't usually go through such a complicated process until he was sure there was serious danger. And if he thought Sophia and Terry were successful experiments, he'd have never let them walk away. He would've sent all of Elemontera after them.

Jack's brow furrowed and he was quiet for a moment. "Maybe. That would explain why I remember some things about them, and some seem almost like a dream." He groaned. "But now they're a threat and Sophia left me with this..." He started toward the computer and pressed a couple of buttons on the keyboard. A moment later, a video of Sophia appeared on the screen.

"I wonder if you still remember me," she said, a grin on her face. "But I'm coming back for you. Your pet killers will be brought down and there will be nothing left of Elemontera or of you after I'm done. I thought tainted elementals would be using their elements for good, but you're turning them into weapons, and I won't let that happen." Her smile twisted and the screen went black.

"So you see, I'd love if you could catch her for me, but even if you have to kill her, it doesn't matter. I already have all I need from the last tests, so I'll have to get back to studying it." He scratched his head. "I remember I was supposed to do it, but somehow... something prevented me from doing it or focusing entirely on it. Well, at least my new protection should be good enough to prevent situations like this."

"This is insane." I leaned on the table. "If Sophia is one of us and doesn't want us to be killers, then what is she trying to achieve by doing all of this? It doesn't make sense."

"Maybe her plan is to raise tainteds against regulars, and then somehow use their forces against Elemontera or what's left of it." Jaiden looked around the lab for the first time, then faced his father. "You're not restarting Elemontera here, are you? I can't let you do that."

"You can't stop me either, or your precious serum will go down the drain."

"Don't worry." I placed my hand on Jaiden's shoulder. "He'll need years before he can start Elemontera again, and by then... there won't be a need for such an organization."

"Keep telling yourself that, darling," Jack said. "People will always want power, and if I can give them what they want without consequences, Elemontera will be stronger than ever."

What had Jack said? That Jaiden needed five doses of the serum? Surely we could get all the serum from him and still have enough time to stop Elemontera from being formed again. For now, we couldn't touch Jack, no matter how infuriating he was, but at least we knew more about Sophia, and finding out who she really was could help us immensely against her.

"What exactly did you show to Sophia that made her dislike tainteds so much?"

"I showed her what Jaiden could do," Jack said. "I expected her to be in awe and try it out, but she... wasn't thrilled about it."

"You wanted to replace me," Jaiden said softy.

"No, of course not," Jack said, but we could all see the lie on his face. That was exactly what he'd been doing, and if he hadn't been mind-controlled by either Terry or Sophia, he would've gone after them and maybe managed to capture them so he could get them to work for him instead of Jaiden.

"Who helped you escape from Jaiden? We know it was a mind controller," I said. "Who else is working with you?"

"I don't... I don't remember that." Jack looked sincere for a change. "All I know is that I was suddenly out and it didn't matter how. Now that I think of it...

everything was so fuzzy. You mind controllers really are a special bunch."

"Yeah, you don't like our abilities when they're used on you, but it's totally fine when they're used on someone else for your benefit."

"Of course." Jack clapped his hands.

"So you have no idea who mind-controlled me and helped you get out?" Jaiden asked.

"No;" Jack said. "But you should be able to figure that one out. That's really none of my concern." His eyes narrowed at Jaiden. "I'm a bit peeved that you intended to hold me prisoner, but get Sophia for me and I'll forgive you."

"Let's get out of here. There's nothing else he can tell us," I said to Jaiden.

"Yeah." He looked at his father. "You're lucky Sophia is a threat to us too, otherwise..."

"You'd do what I say anyway." Jack offered us both a wide smile. "Oh, and if you need help tracking her down, I can offer you some interesting devices."

I seized Jaiden's arm and led him out of there before we both decided to forget everything and just go for Jack's throat instead.

Chapter 13

When we got back to the lab, everyone was there: my parents, Noah, Marissa, Ashley, and Sam. Their faces instantly brightened when they saw us, and my parents sprinted toward me, pulling me into a big hug.

"I was already getting worried Maiers captured you. Please tell me you got rid of him, or that you at least wiped his mind or something," Noah said.

"No." I sighed. "We couldn't touch him because he has something we need, and... he told us something interesting about Sophia."

"Yeah," Jaiden said. "And we have a plan."

"Oh good. Please tell me it's something easy," Noah said, grimacing. "I'm really tired of dealing with people who want to hunt us down."

"Sophia is one of us," I said, and everyone gaped at me.

"She what?" Noah said.

"Impossible." Marissa shook her head. "She's older than us. She can't be!"

"Are you sure Maiers didn't lie to you?" Sam asked. "It wouldn't be a surprise. Did you use mind control on him to know for sure?"

"He's protected against us, so no, but... he showed us a video that Sophia sent to him and she's definitely after him too. Apparently she's one of the adults who were experimented on so they would turn into tainted elementals."

"But didn't all those experiments fail?" my mom asked in confusion.

"Yeah, most of them, but something happened to two of them that made them seem dead, but I guess they weren't, so they're now tainted elementals. Jack said he couldn't recreate the process, but I'm not sure we should believe him." I was getting tired of the whole thing. "But we'll deal with him later. First we have to stop Sophia and then find that other person. Jack says his name's Terry. We should track him down too to make sure he's not a threat to anyone. Jack called him unstable, but Jack is not perfectly sane either, so we can't trust his judgement."

"Whoa, slow down. When did that experiment happen? Jack would've..."

"Not recently. He's been mind-controlled so those two could escape, I guess... I can't heal Jack's mind to check."

"What if he thinks that's what happened but it actually didn't? What if none of what he says is true?" Ashley said.

"Well, someone still had to mind-control him, and even if Sophia isn't one of us, she's working with one or more tainteds, which means our best shot at discrediting her in front of everyone is to film her using her abilities or working with tainteds," I said. If we showed a video exposing Sophia's secret, she'd lose people's support.

"I think she's one of us," Marissa said thoughtfully. "We were watching her and then she just disappeared... well, not like turned invisible or anything, but we suddenly couldn't see her anywhere, so either someone turned her into air and made sure she flew low enough not be seen or she did it herself. The cops actually showed up to try to disperse the crowd and arrest her for disturbing the public peace and for an illegal gathering, but she managed to escape."

"Wait, you were at that gathering. What did she say? Did you see her use mind control on people? If she can do that, she could turn everyone against us."

"No," Marissa said. "We didn't see any shimmering or any signs of one of us with her. She was merely talking about the danger that tainteds represent for our society and said that more should be done to catch the murderers. When the cops showed up, she yelled something about the government being mind-controlled and protecting the bad guys. And she called you and Jaiden cowards for not showing up. The crowd was mostly cheering for her, but only her supporters came, anyway."

"How many of them?"

"Maybe a thousand or so." Marissa cringed. "They were yelling vile things."

"Do you think she mind-controlled them to support her?" Ashley asked. "Could she do that to a thousand people?"

"I don't think she had to do that. Some people actually agree with her," I said.

"But if she's one of us, why rile everyone up? Sooner or later someone will find out about her and tell the press all about it." Marissa's forehead wrinkled.

"Not if she gets rid of Jack Maiers and everyone who knows about her, or if she mind-controls her enemies. Maybe that's why she's not using her elements in public, because then tainted elementals could see her."

"Well, if Jack told you two, then she's not really doing a great job, is she?" Noah said.

"But we don't know when he was mind-controlled," I said. "It could've been while Sophia was still inexperienced with her abilities, or it was someone else. Maybe the same person who mind-controlled Jaiden into letting Jack go."

"What? Someone mind-controlled you?" Noah's eyebrows shot up as he looked at Jaiden.

"Let's not talk about that now," Jaiden said. "We don't know what Sophia is capable of or what her ultimate goal is, but now we know we don't have to engage her, just make sure we catch her when she's being careless and get proof against her."

"Okay," Noah said. "How do we do that?"

"We follow her," I said.

"And how are we going to know where she is unless she announces it?" Sam asked.

"We'll try to track her elemental energy. If she's one of us, that should work," I said. "Jack has some devices that we could use."

"But if she isn't using her elements..." Marissa started.

"She's probably using them when she thinks no one can see her, or at least someone around her could be using theirs. Those elementals who attacked us might be like us, or maybe not. But they were still using their elements, so maybe Sophia doesn't want to use hers because she doesn't want to hurt people or something... if she's telling the truth about that. But elements are probably being used in some form to keep her out of everyone's reach."

"And how are we going to keep ourselves out of the cops' reach?" Noah said. "Especially you and Jaiden."

"We'll have to use disguises," I said. "And we'll have to be very careful with using our elements. And I hope the cops have worse tracking devices than Jack because I'm sure there are tons of energy spikes all over the city now that everyone is upset about this."

"Maybe Sophia does us a favor and announces her next public appearance," Noah said. "That would be so much easier."

"Yeah, but I doubt we'll be that lucky. Just get ready."

"And what if one us could infiltrate Sophia's group and get what we need?" Ashley said. "Surely we could ask around and find out how to join."

"No, she'd be suspicious," I said. "And if she has a mind controller with her or can do it herself, I'm sure she's using it to make sure there aren't any spies in her group. We'll stick to our plan. We don't want to fight her in the open where people could accuse us of being the bad guys. We'll just find a way to expose her, okay? When I find out who that Terry guy is, I'll send you his photo or description so we can look for him too."

Everyone nodded, and Noah looked up at me.

"I met two new tainteds," he said. "They're just kids, but they don't seem like bad people."

"Okay, do they need help or anything?"

"I found them a safe place to stay and taught them how to hide their elements so others couldn't see them, but other than that... I'm not sure what to do with them."

"We'll figure something out later."

"Sure."

"Is there anything we can do to help?" my dad asked, putting his arm around my mom's waist.

"Yeah, since Lily can't help us, I hope you'll be able to track elemental energy once we get the device for it." I knew my parents didn't want to be excluded, but I also didn't want them in danger, so the safest for them was to stay here and monitor energy levels. We needed someone for that anyway.

"Sounds good," my dad said.

"Honey, I know I keep saying it, but please be careful," my mom said.

"I will." I looked at Jaiden. "Let's go. We need to find a good disguise." Actually, we needed it to hide from everyone, not just from Sophia.

"We need weapons too," he said. "I don't want to rely on our elements only to find out we can't use them."

"Do you think she hates us and what she is so much that she wouldn't want to use her own elements, or even that she'd choose to block them somehow?" I asked as Jaiden and I strolled down the hallway.

He shrugged. "I don't know, but we should be prepared for anything."

"Right." I wished I could understand Sophia's mind. Knowing what tainted elementals could do was scary, but couldn't she also see that Jack was the one responsible for everything? Sure, she promised to stop him too, but she didn't mention him in her speeches or ask people to hunt him down. And how had she even sent him that message?

She could have gotten her revenge on him months ago or when Jaiden had unwillingly freed him, but why hadn't she? Was there something she needed from Jack first? And if there was, what could it be? Then again, maybe she only wanted him to see his dream fall apart as everyone hunted down tainteds instead of wanting to become like them.

"What did your father say Terry's last name was?" I asked as we reached the computer.

"Garrly," Jaiden said, settling in one of the chairs next to me.

"Okay, let's see if we have any luck with him." I wasn't overly excited because without Lily's superior equipment, we could only use public searches, and I doubted Terry had a social media profile. Still, maybe he'd gone to college like Sophia or participated in something else. Although, if he'd done it under a different name, we still wouldn't be able to find him.

"We should check Sophia's given name too." Jaiden squinted at the bright screen as I scrolled through the search results. "If we don't find anything, we'll have to ask my father for help."

I groaned. "Yeah, he'll be so pleased about that." Letting go of the mouse, I shook my head. "This is pointless. Even if there's an old address for them, I don't think they'll be hiding there. And somehow I don't think we'd find any family members either."

Jaiden lifted his head. "Then I guess we'll have to use our elements."

"Use them how?" I raised an eyebrow at him.

"My elements are pretty strong right now. I think I could connect to the minds of passersby and check if anyone had seen Sophia after she disappeared from the square. If they don't know anything, they'll just go on with their business, and if they do, they'll approach us, tell us, and forget it ever happened."

"Um, we don't know how much energy that serum gave you, but wouldn't that cause a big spike of energy?"

"Not if we find a way to mask it..."

"Or make sure they can't track us." A slow smile spread across my lips.

"What do you mean?" Jaiden gave me a curious look.

"We're going to send someone to destroy the cops' tracking system. Only one station has it, right? All we need is for one person to disrupt the power grid."

"Yeah, but sneaking into the station is tricky if they have other types of detectors or if the building goes into immediate lockdown."

"That doesn't matter if the elemental doesn't go inside," I said. "Their electricity comes from a power plant. There have to be some wires or something that can be disconnected or destroyed."

"But how do we find those?" Jaiden frowned.

"We can help with that," my mom said from the door.

"You can?" I turned toward her and Dad.

"Yeah."

"Great." I got to my feet so I could free the computer for my mom. "Are you sure this old thing can do all that?"

"Oh, it looks old, but it's good," my mom said.

"Okay then." I faced Jaiden, who stood up. "We should contact Nick about this. Sounds like a good job for him."

Jaiden nodded. "He could definitely cut some wires or cause something to explode."

"Good." It was time to go find Sophia, before she or someone else hunted us down.

Chapter 14

Once we were ready to go, Jaiden and I looked at each other.

"You look... different," I said, staring at his light blue eyes that were looking at me from under a dark green hoodie.

"Good." He offered me a smile, and at least that seemed familiar. "You look fine as usual." He gave me a quick once over. I'd used green contacts to hide my eyes and I'd tucked my long brown hair under a blond, curly wig. My black leather jacket was tightly hugging my body, and my black sneakers and pants were comfy enough in case I needed to fight.

Jaiden took a phone out of the pocket of his dark blue jeans and stared at the screen. "Do I really have to call him?"

"Yeah, we don't have a choice. He's the only one who can get us a photo of Terry. I'm sure he has it somewhere in his old files." It didn't make me happy that we had to rely on Jaiden's father for information, especially when we couldn't make sure that he wasn't being mind-controlled or lying, but there was no other way we could obtain a photo of Terry without losing too much of our precious time. Besides, we didn't even know where to look for it.

"Fine." He sighed, his shoulders slumped, and he lifted the phone to his ear. While he was waiting for his father to pick up, I headed to the computer room to check on my parents.

"Honey, you..." My mom gaped at me. "It's like you're a completely different person."

"I know. Guess the disguise is good." A smile crossed my lips.

"Yep, it's perfect," my dad said, his lips spread into a smile, but there were lines around his eyes that told me he was still worried about me.

"I'll need you to alert me if there are any big spikes of energy," I said.

My mom bobbed her head. I sensed a presence behind me, and turned to see Jaiden at the door.

"We can go, I got the photo."

With a reassuring smile at my parents, I followed Jaiden into the hallway. He handed me the phone and I checked the photo. Terry was a guy with short, curly black hair, and hazel eyes. His dark stubble made him look older than he was. "Any other info on him?"

"My father wasn't really forthcoming." He rolled his eyes. "But Terry should be around Sophia's age, and he doesn't have any family. My father says he didn't care about the rest, so there wasn't anything else in his files."

"Wonderful." But at least we knew who we were looking for... if this guy was indeed working with Sophia and had been another experiment.

"Come on." Jaiden let his air envelop his body. I did the same, and we flew out into the dark, chilly night. After we materialized in one of the allies, my phone vibrated and I immediately answered.

"Hey, it's me," Nick said. "I destroyed the cops' tracking system. Well, I think I did. The power is off and I think it killed the device because there was smoke coming from the inside. I guess most of their devices died." There was a satisfied undertone in his voice.

"Good, thanks. Guess that means we can use our elements more freely now."

"Yeah, but it works in Sophia's favor too. Now she can attack or do something without having to worry about the cops."

"I know." Not that Sophia seemed particularly worried since she had basically paraded all over the square. I had no idea how many people worked for her, but then again, maybe she was mind-controlling them, so of course she could have a ton of followers and didn't have to worry about anything. Her connections could all be a result of mind control rather than some agreements or friendships.

"What should I do now?" Nick asked.

"Stick around. Make sure the cops don't fix the device too soon." I didn't want to count on the device not working if it turned out to be some kind of a super device that could withstand a lot of damage yet still work. Although, if the cops had it, then it was more likely crap and not overly sophisticated. They lacked the funds rich men like Jack had. I ended the call, pocketed my phone, and turned toward Jaiden. "Nick did it. We can use our elements now."

We walked the busy streets, keeping our eyes wide open for anything suspicious. I didn't know if Sophia would appear anywhere nearby, but maybe someone had seen her at some point. Still, finding that out was harder than expected. Since we had to make sure other tainteds who worked for Sophia couldn't see our shimmering threads and cause panic or attack us, we had to be careful with our elements.

As a woman passed close to Jaiden, his arm brushed hers, his shimmering thread slipping under the sleeve of her coat and rushing toward her head. Since she didn't stop, we knew she hadn't seen Sophia. For a moment, I wished we could just read minds, although the idea that someone could do it to me didn't sound appealing at all.

Lowering my shimmering thread to the ground, I slowly led it toward the man who was walking in my direction. He didn't even flinch when my air snuck into his mind, but he just passed by, as if nothing had happened.

Had no one seen Sophia around here or was everyone just passing through and didn't come here regularly?

One girl flinched as Jaiden's element tried to reach her, her hand shooting for her head, and she squinted her eyes. "God!" she cried out, and the friend who was with her placed a hand on her back.

"What's wrong?" the blonde asked, concern flashing across her features. Jaiden immediately withdrew his element.

"I just had the worst headache." She straightened her back. "But it's gone now."

"One of us?" I whispered as we made our way down the street.

"Most likely. She looks the age."

"I really hope your father didn't have any more successful experiments on adults." Especially the Sophia kind of crazy ones.

"Me too."

My phone went off again. "Yeah?"

"There was a spike of energy. Not too big, but enough to be noticeable," my mom said. "Since you answered the phone, I assume it's not you causing the spike."

Jaiden and I had been using our elements, but that shouldn't have caused too large of a spike. "Can you tell me where it was? It might have been us." Maybe Jaiden's improved elements left a stronger spike than before, not that his father had bothered to point out any possible side effects of the new serum.

"I'll send you the map." My mom ended the call and a couple of moments later an image flashed on the screen. Jaiden leaned over the phone, inspecting the map.

"That's two blocks away," he said.

"Yeah. We should check it out." I slipped the phone back into my pocket and we strode down the street, not willing to risk flying and being seen by Sophia's men. We reached a crowd in one of the alleys, a big fire lit at the end. The fire had to be elemental, so that was why it had caused an energy spike. People were huddled close together, and they were chatting very loudly, so it seemed impossible to get through them and reach the fire to see what was going on. Maybe it was just a party or a gathering.

"I'll go check that side." Jaiden pointed to the left, and I nodded. Squeezing myself between two people with beer cups in their hands, I advanced toward the fire, lifting myself up on my toes to try to see over people's heads.

"Thanks everyone for meeting me here." Sophia's voice rang out and everything quieted for a moment. "We must show those taonteds that we're not afraid of them and that we'll protect our city with all we've got. They won't conquer us!"

The crowd raised their arms and cheered loudly, and I clenched my teeth together. If they knew she was one of us... but yelling it out wouldn't do any good, because I was sure I couldn't prove it. And the angry mob would be on me in a second. Elbowing my way through the crowd, I tried to get closer to Sophia, but people were standing too close together.

"I can't stay for long, my friends," Sophia said. "I have important work to do. Those two cowards need to be caught!"

The crowd cheered Sophia's name and I finally pushed my way through, just as Sophia was walking off a small, makeshift stage, hiding in between a group of men, who were probably her guards. Straining my neck, I saw her pulling a black hoodie over her head and walking away while another girl took her place in between the guards. Where was she going? Would she really go anywhere unprotected?

I doubted it, so I pressed myself close to the wall, and as she passed right next to me, her eyes met mine. So close. She was so damn close, and yet I couldn't do anything. The crowd still shouted her name, but they didn't notice her slipping away right under their noses. She went for the main street, and I rushed after her, shoving away any person who got in my way. When I finally emerged onto the street, I spotted her not far from me.

I ran forward, planning to talk to her and maybe pretend to be one of the supporters before revealing myself, because there were still people on the street and I didn't need witnesses who would give Sophia exactly what she wanted. I dashed toward her and got in her path, but as the hooded woman lifted her head, a pair of unfamiliar dark eyes stared back at me.

"Out of my way, child," the woman hissed. "You ain't robbing me. Shoo!"

My mouth falling open, I stepped aside and let the woman pass. Shit! The woman was dressed identically to Sophia and was about her height, but it wasn't her. She must have found some secret passage and switched with this person. Smart, and so damn annoying.

I went back toward the alley, checking every corner for a passage she could've used, but considering she could probably turn into air, maybe she'd made sure no one could see her and then disappeared. The people on the street wouldn't have recognized her in the hoodie anyway or wouldn't have expected to see her just walking alone at night.

A shadow caught my eye and I hurried toward it. If Sophia had been here, maybe Terry was still somewhere here too, because I hadn't seen him leaving with her... unless he'd used a different path since no one knew him as his face hadn't been all over the news. Or maybe he wasn't working with her at all.

"She was here, I'm telling you, man. I saw her!" the man said excitedly and I realized he was talking on the phone. "She's freakin' hot and... so damn amazing." He leaned his hand against the wall of the building in front of him. "No, man, I'm not lying. She was here and held a speech."

Wow, some people really liked Sophia, and one part of me wasn't surprised. She didn't even need mind control to give a bunch of scared people a reason to unite and make them feel like they have a purpose and that they could do something against the threat that was hanging over their heads.

I let my air seep out of me and toward the man. I didn't know for how long he'd been standing there, but maybe he'd seen something. It didn't make me happy that I would be entering his mind without permission and confirm his belief that tainteds lacked control and moral compass, but Sophia's end game might be more dangerous for everyone, and not just tainteds. The man didn't even flinch and kept talking on his phone as I checked his brain signals, which were all untouched.

"Yeah, well, I'm tellin' you the truth. You don't have to believe me." The man scoffed and forcefully ended the call, tucking the phone into his jeans. His eyes were empty as he turned toward me.

"I saw her when she held her speech. Haven't seen her after that," he answered to the question my element asked.

"You won't remember this," I said, and quickly called my element back, disappointed that we were back at square one. Unless Jaiden had found something.

Chapter 15

I ended up back in the alley, but people were still there and it seemed they were having a great time partying after Sophia's speech. Drinks were being served and someone had turned on loud music. Some were dancing... or trying to. As they swayed on their feet, I had to avoid them so they wouldn't spill their beer all over me. I made my way through the crowd, but I couldn't see Jaiden anywhere. When I reached the elemental fire, I noticed that the men who were protecting Sophia were gone now.

After pushing back through the crowd and reaching the main street, I breathed in a big gulp of fresh air and shivered. It was hot in the alley, but here... not so much. I grabbed my phone and pressed the jacket closer to myself. After a few rings, I heard the click on the other end of the line.

"Jaiden?" I said immediately.

"Moira? Where are you? I've been looking all over for you," he said.

"I'm two houses away from that alley where Sophia was." I lounged against the wall.

"I'll be right there."

Putting my phone away, I let out a long sigh. I'd been so close to Sophia and yet she'd managed to disappear again. I should've tried carrying a tracker with me and then stuffing it into her pocket, but I didn't have any handy devices like that. Lily was unable to help and Jack didn't want to. A smile popped up on my lips as I saw Jaiden swaggering toward me.

"Any luck?" I asked.

"Nope. Just a bunch of people who support Sophia's views." His lip curled a little. "I checked their minds, but they were either too drunk to notice where she had gone or how she had gotten here, or they simply didn't care."

"I saw her. She was only a few inches from me. I looked her straight in the eye and couldn't do a thing about it because of the crowd." I pushed myself off the wall because its coldness was starting to break through my jacket and shirt. "I followed her, but... I lost her for a moment while trying to push my way through the crowd, and by then, she somehow switched with another person who was dressed exactly like her."

"Great." He groaned, then put his arm around me. "Maybe we'll have better luck next time."

"I really hope so," I said, because I didn't want Sophia to get her way. We just had to be better prepared next time we saw her.

"Should we fly and see if we can spot anything? If that energy detector is still down..." He gave me a questioning look.

"Okay." We didn't have much to lose. I took Jaiden's hand and we went to a secluded corner where no one could see us vanishing into thin air. As we were flying over the city, I wondered if the government would finally release an official statement regarding tainted elementals. They were awfully quiet and I didn't like that at all.

Sure, they might be after Sophia for disturbing the public peace, but they weren't trying too hard to catch her. And if they couldn't do it, then they should've at least tried to discredit her statements, but no one had stepped up to do that. Maybe they were still trying to see how many supporters Sophia could get before they made a decision, but that was tricky. If Sophia could mind-control people and turn them into her supporters without anyone even suspecting she could be one of us, then she could take control of the whole city. We couldn't let that happen. Not if she threatened to wipe us all off the face of the earth.

"See anything?" Jaiden asked.

"Nope. Just the old, boring city." The lights were flickering underneath us, the sky incredibly dark and looming. People milled around, cars rushing up and down the streets, but there wasn't anything that seemed different or out of the ordinary. There wasn't even a shimmering cloud anywhere, and I wondered if tainteds were now being more careful and avoided using their elements. Our kind had always been hunted by someone, first by Elemontera, and now by Sophia and her supporters. The latter were far more dangerous because anyone could rise against a tainted elemental, and not just a trained agent that could be easily recognized as a potential threat.

"Then let's head back to the lab. Maybe the others had better luck."

"Okay." Jaiden and I had only been to one part of the city, so hopefully the others had noticed something of interest. They hadn't been flying, so they had a better chance of overhearing something helpful about Sophia's whereabouts or future plans.

After making sure no one was following us, Jaiden and I got back to the lab. Marissa, Nick, Ashley, and Sam were waiting for us, and I offered them a small smile when they looked up from their seats at Jaiden and me. They'd dragged more chairs to the computer room.

"Your parents went to sleep," Marissa said before I could ask anything. "They'll come back in the morning."

"Okay." I dropped into an empty chair, my body suddenly feeling heavy, my back hurting. "Did any of you see anything?"

"Not really," Sam said. "Everything was normal and no one even mentioned Sophia or tainteds."

"We ran into one of her gatherings," Jaiden said and everyone leaned forward, their eyes filled with curiosity. "But she managed to escape and we didn't get any useful info out of the others."

"Shit." Nick said. "I was hoping you would at least get something."

"Have you seen or heard from Noah?" Ashley asked.

I shook my head. "Why? Isn't he here? I thought we'd all be here once we were done."

"He didn't come," Marissa said, twisting a strand of her hair around her finger. "We called his cell, but he's not answering."

"What?" I blinked. "Where was he supposed to go?"

"Um, he was investigating an energy spike downtown," Nick said. "But he called me and told me it had been a false alarm. It was just a fight with elements involved."

"Are you sure?" I was at the edge of my seat, my pulse speeding up. If Noah had been mind-controlled, he would've said whatever the controller told him to. "Just because he told you something doesn't mean that really happened."

"We found an article about it on the net, so I guess there really was a fight. There were even some videos uploaded," Ashley said.

"Did he say he wouldn't be coming?" Surely if someone had mind-controlled him, they would've made sure not to raise any suspicion.

"No, he didn't say anything," Nick said. "Maybe he went to check on those tainteds he found. Or he spotted someone new at that fight and has to deal with them."

"But his phone is ringing, right?" I asked.

"Yeah, he just isn't picking up," Marissa said. "He could be busy, so he doesn't have time to answer."

"Did that ever happen before?" Jaiden asked. "He used to not answer his phone back when we…" He bit his lip. "Is he still doing it?"

"Yeah," Sam said. "Sometimes."

"Okay, let's not panic," I said. "If Sophia was in our part of the city with her men, then she probably wasn't anywhere near that fight. Can you track his phone?"

"Not without the right equipment." Nick grimaced.

I was so tired I wanted nothing more than to just fall into bed next to Jaiden and forget everything. Even my eyelids were drooping. "Can you find it? Borrow it?" And by borrow, I meant take without permission and hopefully return later.

Nick looked thoughtful for a moment, but then just shrugged. "I guess I could try."

"Okay, do that, and then try to track the phone. Will someone stay up to keep watch? Because I'm about to fall asleep in my seat." I rubbed my eyes. *Please Noah be fine.*

"I will," Ashley said. "The rest of you can go to sleep."

"Okay, you keep watch and try to reach Noah. Maybe he stayed with tainteds, got tired, and fell asleep before he could tell us he wouldn't be coming." I really hoped that was what had happened. "Nick, you get the tracker. If you don't hear from Noah in three hours or if you track him down, come for us."

They both nodded, and I pushed myself to my feet, nearly stumbling. Yawning, I took hold of Jaiden's arm and dragged him toward the room we'd used when his elements had been waning. The bed was big enough, and we'd moved all the equipment to a corner so it wouldn't bother us but was still close enough and ready in case of emergencies.

"I hope he's all right," I murmured as I settled on the bed with Jaiden, my head resting on his chest.

"He will be. Probably forgot his phone or fell asleep," Jaiden said reassuringly, caressing my hair. "Get some sleep."

I nodded, closing my eyes. If something had really happened to Noah, I would need energy to be able to find him. I just hoped that I wouldn't have to go look for him because he'd be waiting for us here in the morning.

Chapter 16

A knock on the door roused me from sleep and I forced my bleary eyes open. Ashley was standing in the doorway, a worried expression on her face. I immediately sat up, my heart thudding loudly in my chest.

"Noah? Did you find him?" I asked, although I already knew the answer.

"No. We checked that shelter where he took the tainteds, but he's not there. No one has seen him ever since he went toward that spike of energy," Ashley said. "We've tried to contact him, but the phone just rings. I don't think..." Her voice cracked. "I don't think the phone is still functioning. You know that even when the phone is destroyed, the cell tower still searches for it and that's why it rings and..."

"Okay, find the last location where Noah was supposed to be. Jaiden and I are going there." I immediately threw the covers off me, and Ashley nodded, closing the door behind her. Jaiden woke beside me, his eyes bloodshot.

"They didn't find Noah," I said, my voice filled with panic. "We need to go."

"Okay." Jaiden got up, searching for his clothes. There was no time to bother putting the colored contacts into my eyes, so I hoped no one who could recognize me would be out this late. As soon as I was done dressing, I quickly ran my fingers through my hair and looked at Jaiden, who was putting on his jacket.

We rushed into the hallway and nearly toppled Marissa. She was wearing a nightshirt and rubbing her arms as if she was cold.

"Thank God you're up," she said, offering me a phone. "Here's Noah's last known location. Do you think he...?"

"Not now." I took the phone from her and studied the map. "We'll find him, okay?" I met her eyes, and she nodded. There was no other option because I wasn't willing to accept it. Jaiden and I immediately turned into air and rushed out into the quiet night.

We landed in the middle of the street where the fight had happened. The street was now completely empty, not even a stray cat skulking in the darkness. I looked around, trying to find any clues, or anything that could help us figure out where Noah was.

"I see traces of a fight, but that could be from those elementals," Jaiden said.

"Yeah." I could see where the asphalt had broken because of something heavy or perhaps an earth element hitting it, and the grass was singed where fire must have touched it.

"Hey," Jaiden said, and I looked up at him. "See those?"

I followed his gaze, squinting my eyes. There was something metallic on the nearby building. "Cameras?"

"Let's hope they work." Jaiden started toward the building, and I followed, wondering if the cameras were still filming us. We were so worried about Noah that we hadn't even noticed them before. Who knew if they'd recorded us appearing out of nowhere? Not that it mattered if no one actually watched the footage. If those were just security cameras, someone would watch the tapes only if something happened in the building or around it that warranted such a boring and difficult activity.

"I can see an open window," Jaiden said, and I surveyed the building until I spotted the window on the second floor that he was talking about. It was just above the camera and it was cracked open, but it was enough for us to enter. Making sure no one was there to see us and alert the cops, we turned into air and slipped through the gap. Once we were inside the building, we headed down the dark hallway to find the room with the camera footage.

"In here, I guess," Jaiden whispered as he pushed open the door of a small room that looked like storage. I let my fire come out enough to just coat my hand so we'd have a bit of light, but not enough that would alert anyone or that could trigger a smoke alarm or an element detection system. Jaiden went to the computer that was on a small green desk and started it. I looked around and noticed only shelves with stacks of papers. Luckily for us, no password was needed for the computer, and Jaiden easily found the folder with the latest camera footage.

"Oh, look, there's us." I groaned, leaning over Jaiden's shoulder.

"Yeah, let's delete that." Jaiden pressed a couple of buttons and the video was gone. He fast-forwarded through the rest as we both had our eyes glued to the screen.

"Stop!" I yelled as soon as I spotted a person who looked a lot like Noah. Jaiden did as I asked and slowed down the video. We could see Noah walking by, his hands in the pockets of his pants, his eyes looking at something in front of him, but he didn't seem worried. Then he took out his phone and talked for a while, probably with Nick. After that, he went toward the houses at the other end of the street and disappeared from view. Where could he have gone? Jaiden fast-forwarded through the rest, but Noah didn't reappear.

"We should go in that direction," he said. "He had to have found something there or..."

"Yeah." Straightening my back, I took a deep breath. Hopefully Noah would be somewhere around here. Maybe he'd seen some tainteds and was trying to talk to them in their own home or something. Jaiden and I turned invisible and zoomed through the air until we reached an area outside the camera's view, then materialized.

"This is a quiet area," Jaiden glanced at the nearby houses that were mostly in the dark. "And there don't seem to be many people here."

I looked up at the houses. Most of these looked like family homes and private properties with huge yards. Jaiden was right. There were maybe five or six families here. If Sophia had tried to take Noah here, there would've been witnesses, especially if everyone had come out because of the fight. "Who was it that got into a fight? The neighbors?"

"From what I could see on the computer screen behind Ashley's back, it was between the sons of two families here. Something about a car." He scratched his head.

"Then we should go check if anyone here has seen Noah." In different circumstances, I would've waited until morning and maybe tried to start a civilized conversation with someone, but Noah didn't have that kind of time if he'd been taken. It was getting really hard not to use my elements on unsuspecting people.

Jaiden nodded and we started toward the closest of the houses. As we were walking to the front porch, I noticed something dark lying in the grass.

"Jaiden..." I said as I halted, staring at the object, but it was too dark to see it.

"Yeah?" He stopped next to me, his eyebrows going up.

"What's that?" I pointed at the object.

A frown line creased Jaiden's brow and he used his air to lift the object and bring it closer to us.

"Oh God." I covered my mouth with my hand as I realized it was a phone, a familiar looking phone. Jaiden took what was left of it into his hand. The screen had been smashed.

"Is it his?" I asked.

"Probably." Jaiden's face was expressionless.

"Someone attacked him here." I narrowed my eyes at the dark windows, wondering if someone was observing us or if everyone was fast asleep. Could someone have realized Noah was a tainted elemental and had taken him hostage? With our ever-growing list of enemies, we could never know who was after us.

"We should ask someone." Jaiden strode toward the porch, and I followed him. We briefly turned into air so we could pass through the cat door, and once we were in the house, the sound of soft snoring drew us to the room where a man was stretched out on the couch, his arm draped over his stomach, his glasses askew on his nose. The TV was still on, but muted, and a can of beer was lying on the floor, along with a half-eaten sandwich.

Jaiden used his air and slipped his shimmering thread into the man's head. The man's eyes flew open and he sat up, his dark eyes staring in front of him.

"Did you see any strangers around here today?" Jaiden asked. This wasn't an area with many visitors and probably everyone knew everybody, so any new faces would certainly be noticed.

"Yes," the man answered. "A group of people."

"Other people must have come too when they heard about the fight," I whispered to Jaiden, and he nodded.

"Did you see a guy with dark hair and blue eyes? He was wearing a dark blue sweater and black pants," Jaiden said.

The man was quiet for a moment. "Yes."

"What can you tell me about him?" Jaiden's air swirled around the man's head.

"He was looking around for a while. Really suspicious fella," the man said. "I was watching him through the window, but then his friends came and he went with them. Haven't seen him after that."

"His friends?" I asked suspiciously.

"Yeah, they were in a van. Someone waved him over and he got in. They drove off."

I looked at Jaiden, frowning, and he shook his head. What friends? All Noah's friends were currently worried about him or looking for him. There was no one else...

"And he went with them willingly?" I asked.

"Yeah, was smiling and everything."

"Could be mind control," I said to Jaiden. A good mind controller could've reached Noah from inside the car and gotten him to act as if he were happy to see the strangers. But what did they want with him? Had it been someone who worked for Sophia? Did she know he had worked for Elemontera?

"What about his friends? What did they look like?" Jaiden asked.

The man shrugged. "Don't know. It was too far to see and the van was dark."

"What else do you remember about the van?"

"Not much. It was black and big. I wasn't paying much attention to it."

"You won't remember any of this and you'll go back to sleep," Jaiden said, and the man lay down on the couch, closed his eyes, and continued snoring as if nothing had happened. The only difference was that his glasses had fallen off his nose.

"So someone really took him." I swallowed past the lump forming in my throat. "We just don't know who." They must have tossed his phone later, or used their elements to get rid of it so it couldn't be traced.

"We'll find him," Jaiden said determinedly.

"What if Sophia is looking for other ex-Elemontera agents? If she has files about them..."

"I don't know. She hasn't publicly accused anyone of anything, except us." Jaiden frowned.

"Yeah, that's weird."

"Everything about that woman is weird. Maybe she only wants to hunt down tainteds she considers evil and will let others go..."

"Or maybe not." I wasn't about to count on Sophia's humanity. "Now what? Do you think she'll try to use Noah against us? If she wanted him dead, she would've done it already and announced it somewhere."

"I don't think she'd gain anything by actually admitting she killed a tainted elemental," Jaiden said. "She could get away with killing us, but Noah... he's innocent. She has nothing on him except that he worked for Elemontera, and he hasn't really done anything bad."

"She'll use him to draw us out, then." There was an empty feeling in the pit of my stomach. Jaiden's phone vibrated and he answered.

"No, we haven't. He's been taken. No. I'll explain later," Jaiden said. "Yeah, okay. See you."

He ended the call and I raised a questioning eyebrow at him.

"It was Nick. He says the cops will need at least two weeks to fix their systems. There's no sign of Noah anywhere, but we already knew that. Told him we'd go back to the lab."

"Okay." I let my element envelop me, and we left the house and headed back to the lab. Wherever Noah was, I prayed that he was fine. And if he wasn't, whoever had kidnapped him would seriously regret it.

Chapter 17

Jaiden and I looked at each other as we landed in front of his father's new lab. After trying every possible way to discover something about Noah, we gave up and decided to ask for help.

"Oh, there you are," Jack said as he passed through the door, his smile as wide as it could be. "I was wondering when you'd need my help again."

"One of ours has been taken," I said. "If you still have the means to find out who it was…"

"Whoa, Moira, I didn't resurrect Elemontera completely," he said. "But maybe there's something I can do. Not that I care about your friend." He waved his hand. "Come on inside."

I took a deep breath and followed Jaiden and his father into the building.

"You haven't really been successful at solving my problem," Jack said, shooting a displeased look at his son. "I've given you so much power, and yet, Sophia is still walking freely. If you were still in Elemontera, we'd have solved this in less than a day." His mouth curled. "But no, you had to ruin Elemontera, and now look where we are... hiding like rats."

"Oh, what do you know about hiding and rats?" I snapped. "You know full well why there are people after you. It's your own goddamn fault."

"I wasn't talking to you." He sneered and placed his hand on Jaiden's arm. "Now seriously. Why do I have to wait so long? Are you any closer to capturing that woman?"

"Father..." Jaiden licked his lips, and pulled away from Jack's touch.

"No, don't say it," Jack said. "You're absolutely incompetent on your own."

This time a puff of air sent Jack flying down his sparkling clean hallway.

"Moira!" Jaiden said, but he didn't look angry about it. In fact, the corners of his lips were tugging up.

"Sorry, couldn't help it." I shrugged as Jack got to his feet, his eyes shooting daggers at me as he dusted off his clothes.

"Are you trying to kill me?" Jack asked, crossing his arms. "I don't have to help you, you know. It's the two of you who need me!"

"Yeah, yeah." I threw my hands up. "Whatever. But my friend is missing and I'm sorry if I can't listen to your useless yapping right now!"

"Useless yapping," Jack murmured, touching the back of his head and inspecting his hand, but there was no blood.

"Just tell us how you can help us," Jaiden said as we made our way to the computers.

"One of my men managed to get the satellite to work again. Well, partially, but it should be able to get images of the area where your friend was taken. It's been recording everything for the past three days, so if it was filming that area…"

"Good." Jaiden immediately took a seat in front of the computer and started typing something. I assumed he still remembered how to use the satellite from the time when he'd worked for his father. I settled in the chair next to him, watching the screen. Jack loomed over us and I lifted my eyes toward him. He just offered me a twisted smile, clearly not willing to go away and leave us alone with his precious satellite.

"Got it. The van unfortunately disappears because the satellite moved to another area, but it's something," Jaiden said after a few minutes, and I focused on the zoomed image on the screen. It was indeed a black van, and this time we could make out the plates. Jaiden entered the search system that would hopefully tell us who owned the car.

"Who else has satellites that are this good?" I asked Jack. If anyone could film and zoom everything so clearly like this, then we were screwed because there was nowhere to hide.

"Only me, for now," Jack said proudly. "It's the latest technology."

"Great," I muttered. Why do the bad guys always get the best things?

"The van belongs to one Carl Thomasen," Jaiden said. "He lives on Fireby Street." The photo of an elderly man with short gray hair and brown eyes flashed on the screen.

"Know him somehow too?" I glanced at Jack.

"No, never seen him," Jack said, and I hoped he wasn't lying this time.

"Who's the guy?" I turned to Jaiden.

"No idea. Probably some random guy, although he didn't report his van as stolen. Maybe someone mind-controlled him into handing it over."

"Could be, but we still might be able to find out who did that." I could heal his brain or we could mind-control him to tell us what he remembered.

"Yeah. We should pay him a visit."

I jumped to my feet, ready to get as far away from Jack as possible.

"Leaving so soon?" He actually pouted.

"Why? You need company in your hideout?" I asked, my body slowly turning into air. "Why don't you just call one of your men? Or the rats can keep you company."

Jack tsked, and Jaiden and I were out of there before he could say anything else.

"I'm coming with you," Nick said determinedly as soon as Jaiden and I had finished telling everyone that we'd be going to inspect the van owner's house for any clues. We didn't want to waste any precious time, so we all whizzed straight to the house. As we landed onto the porch, I observed our surroundings and slowly materialized. The sky was dark and cloudy, the rain almost ready to fall. The door of the house was locked, and the shutters were closed.

"Maybe he's not here," Nick said. "He could've gone to live somewhere else or he's on vacation, so he left the van here and doesn't even know it's gone."

"Could be," I said. That was a far better option than Sophia's group mind-controlling him or even killing him to take possession of the van. Although, I wasn't entirely sure how far she was willing to go to obtain what she wanted. If she really cared about regular elementals, she would never harm one. "Or maybe he's a supporter, so he gave her the van."

"If it's even Sophia who kidnapped Noah," Jaiden said.

"Has to be," I whispered. If we were dealing with yet another threat, I was going to lose my mind. The porch was hidden behind the trees, so at least no one could see us from the street.

"I don't see any holes," Jaiden said. "We'll have to break in."

"Do it," I said, and Jaiden hit the door with his air, pushing at it until it flew open. We stepped into the dark hallway, and Jaiden searched the wall for a light switch, but when he flipped it, nothing happened.

"Lights are out," he whispered. Either nobody had lived here for a long time and the electricity had been turned off, or someone had destroyed the lights. We stood there in the darkness for a moment. The only thing I could hear was our breathing and the beating of my heart.

"What now?" Nick asked.

I created a small fireball and illuminated the hallway.

"That's nice," Nick said. "And what are we non-fire people supposed to do?"

"Find a candle or something," Jaiden said, his own fireballs illuminating the walls. I picked up a photo from the cabinet and realized it was dusty.

"I don't think we'll find anyone here," I said.

"Yeah, this place looks abandoned," Nick said, then found a small candle in a glass. Jaiden lit it up for him, and Nick grinned. "Thanks."

"Moira, you check the room to the right. Nick, go left. I'll check the back yard," Jaiden said. "Meet me outside later. I doubt you'll find anything interesting here."

He was probably right. The house was small, with only a kitchen, a room, and a bathroom, and I could already tell from here that the bathroom was empty. Slipping into the kitchen, I let my fireballs hover near the ceiling, and headed for the fridge. When I opened it, I saw it was empty. No food or anything that would indicate someone had been here recently.

I checked a few drawers, but they were mostly empty. There was nothing here for us. We were wasting time. Still, since we were already here, it couldn't hurt to check every corner. Crouching, I traced my fingers across the floor. There was no dust or dirt, which was strange. Maybe someone had been here after all... The door slammed shut, making me jump. I sent more energy into my fireballs so they'd be bigger, and then turned toward the door, ready for action.

"Nick? Is that you?" I yelled, just in case it had been him who'd closed the door. Maybe he had been flying outside and the door had closed because of the wind. My shoulders tense, I inched toward the door. But as I pulled the knob, I realized the door was stuck... or locked.

"Hey!" I banged at the door, hoping to catch someone's attention. I slammed my fist harder, but the door didn't budge. Dropping my hand to my side, I listened for any noise, but I couldn't hear anyone's footsteps.

"Nick!" I yelled at the top of my lungs, but I didn't get an answer. Great. I stepped away from the door and glared at it. If it wanted to go down the hard way, it would. "If anyone's out there, don't come near the door!" I wouldn't have yelled a warning if I hadn't believed Nick or Jaiden would come, and I didn't want to hurt them.

Focusing on my fire, I sent a powerful blast at the door, which was strong enough to withstand the first attack, so I increased my energy. The door finally burst outward, bits and pieces of it on fire. I threw more of my fire at it, but used it to catch the flames and extinguish them. Using my air to disperse the smoke, I headed into the hallway and followed a thin trail of light until I reached the exit and nearly bumped into Jaiden.

"What happened?" A frown line creased his brow. "I heard noises and was just about to... Are you okay?" He looked me up and down.

"Yeah, the door closed and got stuck. I had to break it." I couldn't see Nick anywhere. "Is Nick still inside?"

Jaiden shrugged. "I guess. Didn't see him come out."

"Okay, let's go get him. There's nothing here for us." I turned into air and flew back inside, whizzing through the hallway and into the room that Nick was supposed to check.

"Nick?" I called, but there was no answer. Jaiden materialized next to me and used his fire to illuminate the room, which was empty.

"Where did he go?" he asked.

"Maybe he's outside." If he had gone back to the porch, then we wouldn't have seen him. We flew outside, but he wasn't there either. Circling the house, we glided in and out, but there was no trace of Nick. I became corporeal in front of the door and raked a hand through my hair.

"He's not here," Jaiden said, his shimmering thread coming back toward his hand. "I can't sense him anywhere."

I swore under my breath, going for my phone. I dialed the number with shaky fingers. Oh God, not Nick too. But we were alone in front of the house. The phone rang again and again, but nobody answered.

"I'll go check for any hidden doors or traps," Jaiden said, turning into air and rushing inside. A sense of dread filled my stomach as the phone kept on ringing. Someone had taken Nick. I didn't know how, but whoever had locked me in the kitchen had kidnapped Nick.

When Jaiden returned, his face serious, I knew that I was right. Nick was gone too. Someone was playing games with us and watching us constantly. I turned around, trying to spot any shimmering in the trees or in the sky, but I couldn't see anything.

"No," I whispered. Jaiden pulled me into his arms, and I clung onto him.

Chapter 18

I chewed on my nails as Sam and Ashley were arguing about Sophia's intentions. A week had passed without any news or clues about Nick and Noah's whereabouts. We didn't know where to look, and Sophia hadn't made any announcements.

"Maybe it wasn't her," Sam said.

"Yes, it was." Ashley raised her voice. "Who else would just kidnap them without being seen or without leaving a trail? We'd know if there were another Elemontera-like agency out there."

"But what's she doing with them?" Marissa asked. "It's been days! She hasn't contacted us or made any demands. She didn't even turn Nick and Noah over to the cops. What the hell does she want?"

"Maybe she's trying to mind-control them into telling her our location." Ashley said.

"I don't think so," Jaiden said as he strolled into the room. "There are no traces of any intruders or spies around here. And since Sophia is so powerful, she would've had our location in seconds if she wanted it."

"What then? I can't do this anymore!" Marissa was at the edge of tears and Ashley pulled her into a hug.

I dialed my parents' new number. After what happened, I decided to send them to a safe place, and I made them promise they wouldn't tell anyone, including me, where they were staying at.

"Honey?" my mom immediately said. "Is everything okay?"

"Yeah, are you still tracking the energy?"

"Of course, but there isn't anything significant." Her voice sounded worried.

"Okay, keep watching and stay safe. Love you."

"Love you, too."

I ended the call just in time to see a shimmering cloud blasting through the door. Kenna materialized in the middle of the room, her long dark hair flying around her shoulders, her hazel eyes narrowed.

"Where's my brother?" she yelled.

"We don't know," Marissa said. "But we'll find him."

"It's all your fault!" She glared at Jaiden and me. "You let him come with you and you knew how dangerous that was!"

"Kenna..." I said, getting to my feet. "Nick made his decision and he wanted to help. We have to focus on finding him instead of laying blame on someone."

"And you're doing a great job, I see." She crossed her arms. "You just sit here and wait for a miracle!"

"That's not true. We've been looking everywhere all week," Sam said, and he was right. Jaiden had even contacted his father about the satellite, but we hadn't gotten any images of the house when Nick had been taken.

"Obviously not everywhere because you would've already found him!" she screeched.

"Kenna, please..." Jaiden started to say and was thrown back by her air.

"Oh, no, don't talk to me! You keep ruining my life, you..."

"Kenna!" I stepped in her way so she couldn't go for Jaiden. "We're all worried about your brother, and we'll find him. I promise."

"Yeah, you keep saying that." She scowled. "Empty promises don't mean a thing to me. I'm going to go find him myself."

She turned on her heel and made a step toward the door when a beep made all of us look at the computer. Something was flashing on the screen. It was a red line with two words written across it: play me.

"What's that?" Marissa asked, staring at the computer in shock. "I didn't press anything, did I?"

"Looks like someone's hacked into our system," Sam said. "Should we play it?"

"I... I don't know." I looked at Jaiden, who just shrugged.

"Play it," Kenna said.

"Weren't you leaving?" Ashley asked.

"No. Maybe it's about my brother. Play it already!"

"Okay." Marissa's finger hovered over the keyboard and we all inched closer, our eyes focused on the screen. An image of Sophia's face came into view.

"Hello, tainteds," she said. "Oh, don't be so surprised. It wasn't that hard to reach you. I have something of yours."

We exchanged glances, and I wondered if Sophia could watch us somehow, but she was probably just guessing our reaction. Marissa gasped and Kenna cried out as the camera focused on Nick and Noah. They were tied to metal beds, their eyes closed. The camera returned to Sophia.

"If you want to see your friends alive, you will come to Fortery Bridge... number one... in three hours. I'll meet you there and then we can negotiate. I want all of you to come... all of you. If one tainted is missing, I just might do something..." She glanced over her shoulder and the camera lifted to show Nick and Noah behind her. "...to your precious friends. And don't even think about showing this video to anyone because it will self-destruct in twenty seconds and no one will be able to recover it. If I see anyone else, any regulars, the cops, or anyone who doesn't belong to your little group, your friends will suffer the consequences."

The video froze and then vanished from the screen.

"She has them!" Marissa stated the obvious, her face pale. "We have to..."

For a change, Kenna was quiet, her gaze still glued to the part of the screen where the video had been.

"What are we going to do?" Sam asked. "What does she want with all of us?"

"We can't go," Ashley said. "If we do, she's just going to kill us all. It's a trap. It has to be."

"But we can't just let her kill them!" Marissa's eyes were wide. "Maybe she doesn't want to kill us. Maybe she really wants to talk."

"Talk?" Ashley said. "Yeah, right. And tell us what? To hand over Jaiden and Moira to her in exchange?"

"Maybe," I said, rubbing the back of my neck. It made sense. If Sophia got us and turned us over to the cops or even just caught us, her supporters would be happier than ever and maybe she'd gain even more of them.

"We're not doing that," Sam said determinedly.

"We don't know what she wants!" Kenna said. "But if she wants the two of them, let her have them!"

I went over to Jaiden, placing my hand on his chest. "What are we going to do? We can't not go, but we can't put everyone else at risk."

"It doesn't make sense," he said. "If she wanted only us, she would've told us to come alone."

"Yeah, it's a trap. We just don't know what kind of a trap." I sighed.

"Can't we just do something? Alert someone?" Ashley asked.

"Are you insane?" Marissa shot her a glare. "Sophia will know and hurt Noah and Nick!"

Sam worried his lower lip between his teeth. "So we're going? And whatever happens, happens?"

"It looks like we don't have a choice." I clenched my jaw. There was no way I'd let Sophia hurt my friends.

"But if she catches us all?" Ashley clutched her arms to her stomach as if she were in pain.

"She could have done it already. There has to be something else she wants." I frowned. "She might want us to do something for her."

"And what is it that we could do that she can't?" Sam asked.

"Make us look bad in the press," I said.

"Oh, shit," Sam said. "If she's such a powerful mind controller, she'll force us to do things we don't want to and unleash us on the city! We'll be the monsters she wants everyone to believe we are!"

"Where is this Fortery Bridge?" Kenna asked. "We only have three hours!"

"It's on the outskirts of the city," Jaiden said.

"Then what are we waiting for?" Kenna's eyebrows shot up.

"No, we can't just go there and..." Marissa started.

"Sure we can. We're powerful, and together we can make those people pay for taking my brother!" Kenna interrupted. "If Jaiden could fight off Sophia's supporters with one air shield, imagine what we could do!"

"Sophia probably wasn't among them, and neither was her friend Terry," I said. "She could've gotten other elementals or even tainteds to work for her in the meantime."

"She better not mind-control my brother to go against me," Kenna said. "I've had it with that mind-controlling bullshit!"

"We need to be ready for a fight," Sam said. "Should we take weapons? Element-blockers that we could maybe use on Sophia's men?"

"Yes to all of that," I said, taking my phone out and typing a quick text to my mom so she'd know where we were going and so she could send help if we didn't come back in a few hours. No matter what Sophia planned, she couldn't blame us for calling backup if she tried anything other than talking to us.

"How does she even know about all of us?" Sam asked.

"She could've forced it out of Nick and Noah, or maybe she found us in some old Elemontera files." I shook my head. "Doesn't matter. Everyone, grab any weapon you can find. We'll need it." If Sophia wanted a fight, she would get one.

Chapter 19

I materialized as soon as I landed in front of a big panel with a number one written on it. It was right in front of a huge mansion surrounded by tall trees and a high, black fence. Letting go of Marissa, who I'd been carrying with me, I looked around, but I couldn't see anything. Was Sophia waiting for us inside?

"This is... weird," Ashley said. "Are we sure this is the right place?"

"Yeah, this is it," Jaiden said. Sam approached the fence, reaching out toward it. As his finger was about to touch it, the whole fence shuddered and opened, letting us pass into a big garden. A stone pathway was leading straight to the mansion, and on each side of it were perfectly round green bushes and flowers.

"Whoa, I wonder who Sophia had to mind-control to get her hands on this," Sam said, his mouth hanging open as he twirled around to see every part of the garden.

"Do you see any guards?" I asked Jaiden, who shook his head. Where was everyone? I expected Sophia would greet us with her guards or that someone would be watching us, but we couldn't see anyone, which didn't mean there wasn't a hidden camera or that an invisible elemental wasn't hiding somewhere.

But as Kenna stepped on one of the stones, a wall of green light appeared out of nowhere, and she jumped back. "What the hell?"

Sam slowly put out his hand toward where the light had been, and as his fingers glided through what seemed to be empty air, the green light flashed again. "What is that?" He pulled back, staring at his fingers in wonder.

"It looks like some kind of a force field," Jaiden said, taking a step toward it. The glowing, green, see-through wall appeared again, but Jaiden didn't stop moving. He went right through it, and the wall disappeared again.

Ashley crouched and peeked at the bushes. "I don't see the power source."

"It could be some kind of mix of magic and technology," Jaiden said. "It doesn't hurt. Just feels a bit strange, as if you were submerging yourself in water."

"Should we go through?" Ashley gave me a hesitant look.

"I guess." I started forward. The wall didn't seem to be harming anyone, so I went through. My whole body felt heavy for a moment, and the green light appeared again. An idea sprung into my mind. "It's protection."

"What?" Sam asked as he gingerly stepped through.

"I think it can tell if we're tainted elementals. Maybe it detects if there are two types of elemental energy present and that's why it's green." It would explain why Sophia didn't need guards here to check who was coming. This wall could immediately alert her if someone else tried to pass.

The scary thought was that Sophia had gotten her hands on such a device, but maybe it had been here with the house. She could've tweaked it to fit her desires, because the original owner might have used it to keep magic disease carriers away by not letting anyone without an element pass, or maybe to let in only people of a certain element. It seemed like a nice anti-theft protection if only family members were allowed in.

"This better not mess me up," Kenna said. When we were all on the other side of the wall, we strode toward the mansion. As we climbed the stairs that led to the entrance, I kept expecting someone to pop up, but there wasn't anyone.

Jaiden stopped in front of the door, eyeing it suspiciously. "Should we knock or what?"

I was about to open my mouth to answer when the door simply slid open.

"Creepy," Ashley said.

We poked our heads inside, and when we were sure no one was there to attack us, we went in. The foyer was huge, and there was a long hallway in front of us that led to multiple doors and a stairway. The modernly designed furniture was in vivid blue and red colors, and everything was neat and perfectly clean, as if it were just for an exhibition and not for use.

"Sophia! We're here!" Kenna yelled. "Show yourself. I want my brother back!"

"Yeah, I think she knows we're here," Marissa said.

"Then where the fuck is she?" Kenna huffed.

"She's going to let us wait. Wonderful," Ashley said, checking her watch. "Our three hours are up, so I don't know why she isn't..."

The door closed behind us, and before we could react, a gray metal panel slid over every window and over the door.

"Shit! What's going on?" Sam nearly bumped into me.

"The house is in lockdown," Jaiden said. "She trapped us inside."

Kenna used her water against the metallic protection, but her element was simply absorbed into it.

"What's that?" Marissa stammered, and we all looked in the direction she was pointing. A robot resembling a human glided toward us, raising its arms. Snowballs started to shoot out of its arms, and I called to my fire, melting the snowballs before they could reach us. The robot continued firing, and I kept catching the balls. Gritting my teeth, I sent a big blast of fire at it and toppled it over.

"Watch out!" Marissa yelled as a bunch of fireballs came out of nowhere. I ducked, pulling Sam with me, and we hit the floor. Marissa created a wall of water and shoved the fireballs back to the holes in the wall from which they were coming from. Just as the assault ended, Ashley rolled over to avoid the branches that had shot out of the ground and wrapped themselves around her legs. She tried to use her element on them, but the branches wouldn't bend to her will.

Sam scrambled to his feet and used his own earth on the branches, and together the two of them managed to cut them. As I raised my head to see where the others were, Jaiden's air encircled me just in time to protect me from a gush of water that surged from another hole in the wall that I could've sworn hadn't been there a moment earlier.

"What is this place?" Kenna yelled as she fought a burst of water with her own, trying to hold it back. The ground started to shake, and I had to jump up so I wouldn't fall into the hole that had formed.

"No idea!" I said. Fire burst through the opening, almost as if it were a volcano, and I directed my own fire at it. My hands were shaking as I pushed against the force of the fire, and I had a feeling we were fighting against real elements somehow. I just wasn't sure how that was possible.

Soon everyone was trying to fight off the elemental attacks. Jaiden was shooting fire at the snowballs. Marissa was facing a water spurt. Kenna was huddled in a corner, trying to avoid a strong gust of air. Ashley was attempting to gain control over leaves and branches that were constantly shooting out of the ground, and Sam was doing his best to help.

"I can't hold it anymore!" Marissa said. "It's not stopping!"

The fire volcano was still strongly pushing against me, no matter how hard I tried to turn it off. Its energy seemed never-ending. "We have to find a way to shut it down!" We couldn't fight these things forever. Sooner or later our energy would give out, and these things didn't look like they were about to slow down.

"Look for a switch! It has to be somewhere! Or its power source!" Jaiden said. Doing my best to keep the fire in check, I slowly made my way around it and tried to find its source. But it was hard to see anything through the flames. Suddenly the fire changed direction and surged right toward me, shoving me back.

"I don't think this can be shut down from in here," Sam yelled. "There are no switches or buttons or anything!"

"There has to be something!" Jaiden beat down an avalanche of snowballs and turned into air, but as he flew up, he collided with a yellow net that became visible only after he touched it. A cry escaped his lips and he tumbled to the ground. Forgetting the fire for a moment, I used my air to catch him before he hit the ground. Laying him gently onto the floor, I glanced at the fire, which seemed to have ceased for a moment.

"Guys, did you try not fighting it?" I asked, and Sam looked at me as if I were crazy.

"That would be a terrible idea," Marissa said. "These things would... kill us."

"The fire stopped blasting me while I..." Another surge of fire made me yelp, and I quickly used my own element against it. "Scratch that, I was wrong."

"Someone is controlling it," Jaiden said through his teeth as he got up. The snowballs had stopped, but only until Jaiden regained his balance. Then he had to fight them off again.

"She's toying with us!" Kenna yelled.

"That's why there are no switches. She has to be controlling this from another room," Marissa said.

"But why?" I couldn't understand Sophia's actions. If she wanted us dead, she wouldn't have stopped the attack until we regained our strength or composure, or would she?

"I don't know," Marissa said, struggling against the water. "But I can't..."

The wave of water became too much and it slammed into Marissa, washing her down the hallway, toward one of the rooms.

"Marissa!" I yelled, but before I could use my air to try and catch her, a blast of wind made me press myself against the floor and cover my head. As the wind died down, I lifted my eyes and saw Sam being dragged away by a long vine. Ashley screamed as branches wrapped around her wrists and ankles and tossed her aside.

I lifted myself up, avoiding the fire, but a surge of water slammed into me. Pain erupted through my body, black spots dancing in my vision as I fought to breathe. My back hit the wall, and I could hear Jaiden yelling my name. The sounds were muffled as something picked me up and threw me through a door. I slid across the hard floor, my wet hair plastered to my forehead.

Blinking, I tried to clear my vision. When I was sure the strange force that had carried me wasn't around anymore, I took a slow breath and pushed myself up. The door closed with a thud, some kind of a yellowish glow appearing over it for a moment and then vanishing. I was sure that if I touched it, it would turn yellow again.

The room I was in was small and completely empty. There weren't any windows or exits. The walls were painted with colorful lines, stylish swirls, and unidentifiable shapes. Even the floor was ornamented with black circles and flowery symbols.

Suddenly the whole room started to shake, and I stopped in the center of it, standing right over a black circle. Something was going to come out of the wall. I was sure of it. The only thing I didn't know was if I could survive and defeat it.

Chapter 20

A bright white light blinded me for a moment, and as I squinted my eyes, the wall in front of me parted and two big metal flowers surged out. Before I could see what they really were, fire and air started gushing out of them, creating a blue fire for a moment. I called to my air and created a shield, but the force of the fire and air slamming into it pushed me a couple of steps back.

"Sophia! What do you want from me?" I yelled as I shoved my energy at the flower-like devices. No one answered, but the elements coming toward me increased in their strength. Sweat trickled down my back, and slow tremors started to spread all over my body. As soon as my elemental energy touched the metal flowers, it was as if someone had sucked out all of my strength.

What were those goddamn things? How did they even work? Dropping the shield, I threw myself to the ground and rolled over as the flowers changed the direction of their attack. They were following my every movement. I couldn't keep this up. There was nowhere to run. The more energy I used, the quicker I got drained, while the attacks only grew stronger. Were my elements feeding them? Were they using my elemental energy to attack me? Shit.

I turned into air, hovering just above the ground. If I rose up, I was sure I'd collide with a yellow net similar to the one Jaiden had run into. Gliding right and left to avoid the attacks, I tried not to engage the flowers. Dodging the fire and moving swiftly, I drew closer to the wall with the flowers. If I could somehow get behind them or get them to turn the energy against themselves...

Fire caught my shimmering arm and pain shot up my shoulder. I hadn't been quick enough to part my air around it, so it had burned me a little. Hissing, I quickly materialized, inspecting my arm, but aside from the slight redness of my skin, I didn't see any burns. The flowers were turning toward me, so I gathered my strength and turned into air, rushing at them. I hovered in between them, bracing myself. When they turned toward me, I surged up so fast that I was dizzy. I made sure not to go too high so I wouldn't collide with the net.

The flowers sprayed each other with elements and I closed my eyes as they burst into flames, smoke filling the room. I landed, materializing, and waited to see if the flowers would recover, but they didn't. Wiping the sweat off my forehead, I took a shaky step toward the wall. The flowers were no longer in their original shape. Now they looked more like huge metal heads with spaghetti on them.

I peeked inside one of them and saw a pipe that was leading somewhere, but I didn't have time to go investigate. I had to leave this room and get everyone else out of this place.

As I turned around, the yellow light flashed across the door. Right. My exit was blocked. Rolling my shoulders, I tilted my head to the side. The door was going down no matter what. I'd had enough of this madness. I sent a small fireball at the door, and the yellow light easily consumed it. It seemed that no matter how strong I attacked, the door would simply absorb my elements. My energy was already low from all the fighting. I couldn't afford to lose any more, not after I'd defeated Sophia's stupid robot flowers, or whatever they were.

I stepped in front of the door, placing my fingers against the light, which glowed stronger, but I could feel the wooden surface through it and I didn't feel any pain. If I was right, this was only elemental protection. A slow smile spread across my lips as I kicked at the door. Nothing happened, so I lifted my leg and tried again. If only I had something to throw at the damn thing. My eyes fell on what was left of the metal flowers. I dashed across the room and kicked them until they detached and fell to the floor.

Their metal heads were heavy, and I couldn't lift them up by myself, but I could certainly use my air to do it. The door would only absorb my elements if they touched it, not if I used them on something else. Summoning what was left of my energy, I wrapped my air around the metal heads and threw them at the door. Shielding my eyes, I could see the heads forming a huge hole in the door, so I sprinted for it and immediately pulled myself through the gap. When I was out, I looked down the hallway.

Kenna was just emerging from another room and scowling at the burning door.

"Are you okay?" I asked.

"Yeah." She patted her jacket. "I'm so glad I brought grenades with me. What the fuck is this place?"

"I've no idea. Let's get the others." I kicked at the nearest closed door. "Do you have any more of those grenades?"

"Yep." Kenna tossed one to me and I caught it. The grenade was the size of a Ping-Pong ball, its surface smooth and bluish. Pulling out the trigger to activate it, I hit the door once again and it opened without trouble. It seemed like it was much easier to get in than get out. I spotted Marissa cowering on the floor.

"Stay down!" I yelled and hurled the grenade at the flowers. Small explosions rocked the mansion, and Marissa came running toward me, her face stained with tears.

"Oh thank God! I thought I was going to die!" She threw herself into my arms.

Sam and Ashley were with Kenna, their faces covered with soot and dirt. The only one missing was Jaiden. There was one room left, but the door was open. As I peeked inside, I realized it was empty.

"Where's Jaiden?" Marissa's chin trembled. "Please tell me they didn't take him too."

Not even willing to consider that possibility, I headed to the foyer. Jaiden was strong. He could've fought off the flowers or anything else that had come at him. I stopped dead in my tracks as I reached the main door. The metal panel was nowhere to be seen, and all the windows were open.

"What's going on?" Sam asked.

"I don't know. Let's get out of here." I bolted for the door and burst through it. Jaiden was lying in the grass, his eyes closed. I nearly tumbled down the stairs as I hurried to him.

"Jaiden!" I yelled. He didn't even stir, but his chest was moving up and down, and I took that as a good sign. Kneeling next to him, I put my hand on his cheek and gently shook him. "Jaiden, hey."

His eyes fluttered open and he looked at me. "What's..."

"Thank God." I briefly closed my eyes, pulling him toward me.

"Is everyone safe?" he asked, sitting up.

"Yeah." Everyone seemed shaken and exhausted, but we were all safe and sound, which is what mattered most.

"Sophia's not here," Kenna said. "If this was her plan to get us killed, then my brother is already..."

"No, don't say that." I met her dark eyes. "I don't think this was meant to kill us."

"Then what was she trying to do?" Ashley asked. "Because this was way too close."

"Maybe it was a distraction," I said. "We were trapped here for at least an hour! If Sophia's in the city, she could've done whatever she wanted and we weren't there to stop it."

"Shit." Jaiden ran his hand through his hair. "We have to go back to the city! Maybe it's not too late. We should send all tainteds to a safe place until this situation is resolved. We can't let Sophia win this!"

"We'll go, but we're not strong enough to fight," I said, flexing my fingers. If Sophia's plan had been to indispose or weaken us, well, it worked like a charm. "Those pipes and holes through which we were attacked... they lead somewhere. If we follow them, we might find the source and Sophia's hiding place."

"We don't have time for that," Jaiden said. "I doubt she's hiding anywhere here. The pipes probably lead to the source of elemental energy and nowhere else."

"Can you carry Marissa and Sam with you?" I asked.

"Yeah," he said.

"I'll take Ashley." I turned toward Kenna. "Let's go."

When we were all just shimmering clouds, we flew as fast as we could toward the lab. While we were moving above the city, we didn't see anything suspicious or any signs of any kind of disturbances, which didn't necessarily mean Sophia hadn't made her move already. Once we were safe in the lab, I dropped into the nearest chair and leaned my elbows onto my knees.

"There's no sign of any disturbance," Sam said, checking the computer. I found my phone and texted my mom. A reply came almost a second later, and she told me nothing had happened while we had been away.

"What the hell was she doing? Having a secret mission?" I frowned.

"Maybe she was relocating Noah and Nick to another place or using them to do something for her that no one other than us could have detected," Marissa said.

"I'm dead on my feet." Ashley yawned. "Can we get some rest?"

"Yeah, you go. I'll keep watch for now," Jaiden said. As everyone trailed out of the room, probably happy that they were able to get some rest, I looked up at Jaiden. He was eyeing the room as if there was something hidden in it. When he caught me watching him, a smile spread across his lips.

"Are you okay?" I asked. "How did you escape the mansion?"

"Yeah, I'm fine," he said. "My energy was too much for those devices. I flew outside as fast as I could, but I got dizzy and I guess I fainted."

"I'm glad we all got out of there alive." I stretched my achy muscles.

"Yeah, but we should really take tainteds somewhere safe until Sophia is dealt with," he said. "I think I know a place where we could gather them to make sure no one reaches or tries to harm them."

"What are you talking about?" I raised an eyebrow at him. "How would we even find all tainteds in the city when we don't even know who they are? And why would we do that? There isn't a place that we can protect effectively. They'd be like cattle waiting for slaughter. It's better they're not in one place."

"We're scattered all over the city now, and look what's going on. We can't catch one woman," he spat out. "If we call out to all tainteds, they'll come. We can face Sophia together, and then she won't be able to take a single one of us."

I narrowed my eyes at him. "I'm not sure about that. It sounds like a bad idea. Tainteds are not fighters. They would be scared. And where is this safe place you keep mentioning?"

"I could show you," he said. "But believe me, it's a good one."

"Um, yeah, okay." My brow furrowed. "Maybe after we find Noah and Nick."

"No, if we wait, Sophia could end up taking more elementals and mind-control them into doing things for her. If we don't act now, it'll be too late." Jaiden's voice was full of urgency.

"Are you sure you weren't mind-controlled?" He wouldn't tell me what kind of safe place it was or where it was located, and he'd never talked about anything with such fervor. Not to mention that his idea had been so sudden and unexpected. Considering what Sophia could do and the fact that he'd been unconscious... someone could've mind-controlled him to think this was what he wanted.

"I wasn't mind-controlled. Check my mind if you want."

"Fine." I gently slipped my element inside his head and he grimaced. All the signals were white, but as I tried to grasp one of them, he shoved me out.

"Hey, you checked, and everything's fine. Can't you just trust me on this? I don't want anyone to overhear our plan. If Sophia could've hacked into our system, who says she didn't do something to be able to listen in to everything we say in here?" His face was serious.

"Right."

"Can you get me something to drink, babe? My mouth is dry." He coughed, offering me a smile. There was something in his eyes... something different that I couldn't put my finger on. It was as if I were watching a stranger through Jaiden's eyes. And he'd called me babe; something he had never done.

"Sure." I got to my feet, glancing over my shoulder as he busied himself with the computer. When I passed through the door, I slammed it behind me so hard that it almost cracked.

Chapter 21

My hands were shaking as I filled a plastic cup with water. Was it possible to mind-control someone into thinking they were talking to a certain person when in fact they weren't? Could someone have mind-controlled us to see Jaiden with us when it wasn't really him? Everything was off about him, and as I carried the cup to the computer room, I knew I was about to find out for sure. Jaiden would be at least a little shaken because I'd closed the door and left him alone in a small, closed space. Maybe the computer would distract him, but probably not completely.

Since the door was still closed when I reached it, I hesitated before entering, but then I took a deep breath and went inside. Jaiden offered me a wide smile as I handed him the cup.

"Thank you." He took a big gulp. His shoulders were completely relaxed, his eyes calm. And as he lifted his gaze toward me, I was sure that real Jaiden would never give me such a contemptuous look. Oh God.

"You know what?" I said. "You're right. We should protect tainteds first. Noah and Nick are important and we have to find them, but we can't risk Sophia kidnapping anyone else."

"I knew you'd come around." Jaiden spread his arms and I walked into his embrace.

"I only had to think about it." I forced myself to smile and wrapped my fingers into his hair... someone's hair. If this wasn't Jaiden, and if I attacked him, we'd never figure out what their plan was, and I didn't want this person to mind-control me if he or she turned out to be more powerful than me. His gaze focused on my lips and I bent my head, closing my mouth over his so he wouldn't suspect anything. When I pulled away, those unfamiliar eyes stared back at me in amusement.

"I'm going to tell the others about our plan." I let go of him and pushed myself up. "But after I get some sleep. Will you keep watch?"

"Yeah, get some rest."

"See you in the morning. Let me know if something happens."

"Will do."

I flashed him one more fake smile and strolled out of the room. There was no time to sleep. I had to go find everyone and talk to them now, before the person who'd infiltrated our base did something to harm us. But as I closed the door behind me, I slid down to the floor, wiping my mouth with my hand.

Letting my air out of me, I risked guiding it into my own mind. With my eyes closed, I blocked out every thought until I was sure my brain signals were untouched. I blinked at the empty hallway. My brain was fine. Who the hell had I kissed? Where was Jaiden? Swallowing past the lump in my throat, I slowly breathed in and out until I was strong enough to get to my feet.

When everyone was on the roof, their faces varying from sleepy to grumpy, I stepped into the middle of the group. "We have a problem."

"Did you find my brother?" Kenna immediately asked.

I shook my head. "Jaiden... he's not... Someone is pretending to be him," I blurted out.

"What?" Kenna scowled. "You woke us up and called us here just to tell us..."

"I'm serious, Kenna," I snapped. "The person who came back with us isn't Jaiden!"

"What do you mean?" Marissa blinked at me, tugging her coat tighter around herself. "Do you think he was mind-controlled?"

"No, he wasn't. He let me into his mind to check and kicked me out before I could do anything else."

"That's typical Jaiden," Sam said.

"No, it's not. He looks... different and isn't acting like himself. I know it's not him. And he keeps insisting on gathering all tainteds and taking them to some place only he knows about. He claims he doesn't want to tell me the details because he thinks we're being watched," I said. "But why would he say anything at all if he was truly afraid of that? If Sophia hears we were rounding up taToronto, she'd make sure to stop us, even if she didn't know where that place was. She'd do anything to find out. His plan is just too sloppy. I agreed with him because I was afraid he could mind-control me, and then we wouldn't have even known it."

"That doesn't make any sense," Sam said. "How could someone look exactly like Jaiden? Were we mind-controlled into thinking it's him?"

"I don't think so. I checked my mind and I didn't see any traces of mind control." Although, if someone had been counting on me to check, could they have mind-controlled me into seeing both mine and Jaiden's mind as untouched when they actually weren't? "If it was just mind control, I don't think he'd lose his biggest phobia or act so differently... I..."

"So you're saying there's a person who can make himself look like another?" Ashley's voice was filled with suspicion. "Are there really such good disguises that we wouldn't notice the person is wearing a mask?"

"I don't think it's a costume or a mask... It's... It feels real." That kiss had certainly felt like touching real flesh.

"Are you sure you haven't been mind-controlled into becoming a paranoid freak?" Kenna crossed her arms.

"Yeah, I'm sure. Sophia or someone wants us to take tainteds to some place. I don't know how she's doing it, but..." I ran my hand over my face. "All I know is that the person with us isn't Jaiden."

"Wait, do you think it could be her?" Kenna asked. "Sophia? Could she somehow pretend to be Jaiden by projecting some sort of a mask?" She turned on her heel. "I'm going to kill that bitch!"

"Kenna!" I had to use my air to create a wall in front of her to stop her from doing something stupid. "Even if it is her, we can't let her know we figured out she's not Jaiden."

"Why the hell not? She's here and alone. We can catch her and get her to tell us where Nick and Noah are. Maybe even trade her for them!" Kenna insisted.

"Yeah, we could do that, but we don't know the extent of her abilities. If she can actually turn into another person... then we can't be sure of anything! If we attack and fail, we'll never find out what her real plan is! And she might even mind-control us so we won't even know what's going on!"

Kenna let her hands drop to her sides, her face troubled. "Then what? Should we pretend everything is fine?"

"Sort of," I said.

"And if it's not her and it's one of her accomplices?" Ashley asked. "We could walk straight into a trap."

"We already have. She managed to switch Jaiden for whoever... There's definitely someone who can change shape and become someone else, and Sophia is the prime suspect. When I was following her, another person appeared there instead of her, and I couldn't understand where she'd gone. She might have slipped through some hole, but it's possible she just changed her appearance, and that was why she wasn't scared anyone would try to stop her, follow her, or recognize her. That would explain how she can just disappear and not be caught or seen. And there was a witness who said Noah had gone off with a friend... Well, maybe he did. If she turned into one of us..."

"Oh God." Marissa's mouth was hanging open. "That's... But then she can get to the president, kidnap him, and pretend to be him!"

"Wait, how would shapeshifting even work?" Ashley paled. "Please tell me she doesn't need a body to animate..."

My stomach clenched, and I swallowed bile. No, Jaiden wasn't dead. I refused to even think about it. "I don't know. Maybe she just has to see that person..."

"Then why hasn't she already claimed the body of an influential person to get what she wants?" Sam asked.

"Probably because she wants all the glory for herself and not for another person. She wants it to be her who gets everything." Or she wouldn't have shown her face all over the news. No, Sophia wouldn't be satisfied just with taking another person's identity.

"How do we even stop someone like that?" Marissa asked.

"I don't know. We get all the weapons we can and make sure our elements stay strong."

"Will we have to bring some tainteds with us?" Sam asked.

"No, it'll be just us." I didn't want to drag any tainteds into this, especially if they didn't have experience with fighting with their elements. "We might get a chance to confront her or whoever it is once we get to that place."

"What if we get mind-controlled there? We won't be able to do a thing." Ashley rubbed the back of her neck.

"And how are we even going to know we are truly who we say we are?" Marissa's brow furrowed. "We have to spend a night or more with this person! If she takes the shape of one of us..."

"We need a secret word. Something no one will be able to figure out," I said.

"That won't help if she can mind-control it out of us," Sam pointed out.

"We have to figure out how to work around that." I didn't know what else to do. Involving someone else was complicated, especially because not many would be able to stand against Sophia and her followers.

"How many people can do that? If it's more than just Sophia..." Marissa's voice quivered.

"Jack said only Sophia and Terry were the experiments who returned from the dead, or survived, or whatever. I'm not excluding the possibility that he might have been lying, but it's possible that the experiment gave Sophia and Terry unique abilities." If there were more of them, I couldn't even begin to imagine the chaos the world would end up in. Mind control and killing with one thought was already scary enough... taking on another person's appearance... that was truly terrifying.

"Yeah, let's hope so." Sam ran his hands over his arms.

"I still don't get why she's doing this. She could've taken all of us..." Marissa said.

"Maybe that's exactly what she's doing, Nick, Noah... now Jaiden..." Kenna said. "Who says she won't kidnap another one of us? Hell, if Sophia is at the lab pretending to be Jaiden, then what if Terry is pretending to be one of us? That would really bust all of our plans." Her eyes darted from one person to another. "Since you came to us with this weird story, maybe it's you." She pointed her finger at me.

"Yeah, how do we know you're really you?" Sam said.

"Ask me anything that you told me or I told you, or I can tell you about the things we've been through together," I said. "Sophia failed to fool me, so that means she doesn't have access to Jaiden's mind. At least not completely. Even if she mind-controlled some details out of him, she still doesn't know him well enough to be able to convincingly act like him all the time."

"Okay, so how are we going to do this?" Sam tilted his head.

"I could mind-control you. Then you'd use our secret word if someone else mind-controls you, and it could be used to confirm your identity too. I would make you forget the word until someone messes with your head. Then you'd come to me and tell me the word or give me a sign." I had no idea if Sophia was planning to mind-control any of us, but we needed to be cautious.

"Fine, but what about you?" Kenna asked. "Are you going to mind-control yourself?"

"I can't do it to myself, so I guess we'll have to take a risk with me. I have higher chances of defending myself against another mind controller since I'm one too."

"So does Jaiden, and look where..."

"Just observe me carefully, okay?" I said. "You'll figure out if I'm acting weird or suddenly agree too much with Sophia's plans."

"Okay, so how do we do this?" Sam asked. "If we just revealed our plan to the enemy..."

"You all look fine. Not like Jaiden," I said. "But you'll come to me one by one, and we'll do a little test to see if you and I both remember some things from our past that no one else could know. Once that is done, I'll mind-control you so you don't end up following anyone's orders." Entering my friends' minds wouldn't be the easiest thing in the world, but I didn't want to lose them or give Sophia any power over them.

"But if she's like you, she might be able to override or erase your mind control," Ashley said.

"I know, but many taulnteds don't know how or haven't even tried to heal anyone's mind, so let's hope she doesn't know about this." It wasn't foolproof protection, but it was something. "Oh, and one more thing. Find small cameras that we can attach to our clothes. If we want to expose her for who she really is, we need evidence. But make sure the cameras are undetectable and aren't connected to anything. We don't want her or anyone to find out about them."

Sam nodded. "Okay. Let's do this."

Chapter 22

I was sick to my stomach when I had to look fake Jaiden in the eyes once again. "Are we going to that place you told me about anytime soon?"

"Yeah, did you tell everyone what they're supposed to do?" the impostor asked.

"Sure. Once you show them where to go, they'll go to the city and gather all the taicnteds they can find," I said, trying to keep my voice steady. "And then they'll guide them to your safe place. I hope it isn't far."

"No, it's not too far." The impostor got up from the chair he/she had been sitting in. Jaiden's lips twisted into a smile so unlike his that it took all my effort to smile back.

"Good. Then just tell us when we can go." Spending days around the impostor while not knowing what had really happened to Jaiden was driving me crazy, but I had to stay strong. Sophia wouldn't tell me where Jaiden was anyway. Well, at least not yet. I'd find a way to get it out of her as soon as the opportunity showed. One part of me wondered if she was the one looking at me from behind Jaiden's dark eyes.

"We can go right now, actually."

"Okay. I'll tell everyone." I headed for the door. The impostor hadn't tried to contact anyone while staying with us. I'd made sure to check the computer and the room for any hidden devices, but I couldn't find any. Unless they were kept in Jaiden's clothes. Marissa, Ashley, Sam, and Kenna looked up at me when I approached, their eyes filled with anxiety.

"We're going today. Get ready." I gave them all a meaningful look, which meant they should find as many weapons as they could and hide them so the infiltrator couldn't see them. If we ended up trapped in anther place that could block magic, we'd need something that could help us break out without a problem.

"Do we really have to let Sophia or whoever it is carry us with her air?" Ashley asked, her eyes wide.

"Yeah, just like you would let Jaiden."

She pressed her lips into a tight line, but she probably knew we had no choice other than to pretend everything was fine. If we were going to play this game, we had to play it right.

We were flying above the endless fields until we reached a small village just outside the city. The impostor led us straight to a big farm, but as we landed and materialized, I noticed there was a metal construction in the middle of it. As we came closer, I thought it looked like a silo. Its metallic blue walls reflected the sunshine, and it seemed like it had been built recently.

"How do you know this place?" I asked the impostor.

"From my Elemontera days. It's an old lab, but no one's been using it for a while."

"That's not big enough for many tainteds," I said. "It's high, but too narrow."

"No, it's not. The main part is underground." A smile crossed Jaiden's lips.

"Oh, okay then. But are you sure this is safe?" I couldn't exactly just smile and nod because that would be suspicious. "If your father knows about this, we're going to have a problem. He's already trying to create a new Elemontera, so how come he's not using this?"

"Don't worry. He won't be coming here. This place is too far from the city. He'd risk getting caught out here, and it's hard to smuggle things from the city that he needs without being seen. Large trucks are too obvious and he doesn't have tainteds anymore to do his dirty work for him."

"Can we take a look inside?" I eyed the rest of the farm, but I couldn't see any people hiding anywhere. Ashley, Kenna, Sam, and Marissa were standing behind me, probably too afraid to come closer.

"Of course." Jaiden's hand extended toward me and I had to take it. We all made our way across the dry grass and reached the metallic door. The impostor let go of me and placed a hand against the shiny screen at the door, which swirled with white and green, and then opened. White and green? Air and earth, maybe? Sophia? Was Sophia the one hiding behind Jaiden's face? Terry had water, so the lights would've been blue, if that was how the elemental lock worked.

The impostor stepped aside, waving his hand to indicate that I should go inside first. Bracing myself, I entered a small, dark, windowless room. There were various panels on the ceiling that were releasing a light yellowish glow. Most of the equipment was covered, but on the ground were pipes similar to those we'd seen in the mansion. Actually, as I looked at the plain walls, I suspected this place was working on the same principle as that mansion.

"You can all go look around." Jaiden's voice broke the silence. "When you're done, head immediately to the city and find as many tainteds as you can. Moira, stay with me. I want to show you something."

Marissa gave me a quick look, and I inclined my head when the impostor wasn't watching me. They followed the narrow hallway toward what look like another room, but the impostor and I stayed behind.

"What is it that you have to show me?" I asked, keeping my voice soft and light.

The impostor's eyes observed me carefully. "There's enough room here for many tainteds, but I thought we could use our own special space."

"Oh?" My eyebrows shot up.

The impostor lowered a latch and one of the panels on the ground moved, revealing a stairway that led into the darkness.

"Go on."

I carefully stepped into the darkness, half-expecting to be pushed and have the door closed shut behind me, but the impostor followed me downstairs. Something beeped, and light filled an empty room.

"I didn't buy any furniture yet, but..."

I turned around, checking every corner, but I didn't see any strange devices in here. Wherever Sophia had taken Noah, Nick, and Jaiden, this wasn't it. I hadn't even spotted any guards or anyone. Deciding I had nothing to lose since there wasn't anything here that could tell me why Sophia wanted all tainteds in this place, except maybe to trap them, I turned toward the impostor and enveloped my arms in fire. I couldn't go another second without knowing where the real Jaiden was.

"Who are you?" I asked, ready to unleash my element at the slightest movement.

"What do you mean, Moira? Are you okay?" A frown creased Jaiden's brow. "It's me. Did something happen?"

"You're not Jaiden." My voice was low and edgy. "Don't try to deny it."

"How can you say that? You know me. What's gotten into you?"

"Show yourself!" I'd had enough of this, so I blasted my fire at the impostor, who immediately turned into air and evaded my attack.

"Well, well, Moira." A familiar female voice rang out. "What gave me away?"

"Everything." I didn't wait for Sophia to materialize. Instead, I sent a gust of air toward her to try to destabilize her.

"Bravo! You've figured me out. Do you want an award?" She became visible not far from me, her lips stretched into a smile, and I was glad she was back to her true form. "Sadly, no one will ever find out about it."

"How are you doing that? Changing into other people?" I let my air shimmer in front of me in case she tried anything.

"Ah, little Moira. Some of us are more powerful than you could ever imagine." She disappeared and flashed in front of me within a second, and when her air crashed against mine, my shield gave.

"Then why are you hunting us? You're worse than anyone else. You're going against innocent people of your own kind." I rolled to the ground to dodge a gust of air aimed at my head.

"I'm merely trying to help people!" Her eyes flashed dangerously and she took a step toward me. A branch appeared out of nowhere, wrapping itself tightly around my neck.

I coughed and spluttered, grabbing at the branch, but it was too strong for me to break. Focusing on my fire, I let it surge through my neck. "Help? You're insane. How is hunting down tainteds and turning people against each other helping anyone? We'll end up killing each other! You even called for war!"

"Sometimes you have to make sacrifices to achieve the things you want."

"Yeah, I heard a madman or two say that." I called to my fire and flung blue fireballs at her. She dodged all of them, but one caught her on the arm, unbalancing her briefly.

"You don't understand anything," she hissed.

"No, I don't. Where are my friends? What did you do to them?" I blasted her with my air, but before her back hit the wall, she became invisible and shimmered away from me.

"Don't worry. They're not dead yet. I just needed to familiarize my element with their bodies so I could use their likeness." She became corporeal in the corner of the room, but as I threw more fireballs at her, thin branches formed a net in front of her, and my fire crashed against them, barely having any effect.

Gritting my teeth, I found my air again and started a powerful blast, spinning it until it formed a small tornado. Sophia met it with a tornado of her own, and our forces clashed, the elements exploding and throwing us both backward. My head hit the floor, and black spots danced in my vision.

"Surrender. Now. And I won't hurt you... much." Sophia appeared over me, and I had only enough time to raise my hands to shield my face from her air. I sent my own air out, but she didn't budge. Her hair was flying wildly around her, her brows drawn in concentration. Her air somehow found its way to my throat, choking me. I rolled over, kicking out with my leg and bringing her to the ground.

The pressure in my throat started ceasing, and I let my fire consume my body. As I got up, Sophia glared at me. With one flick of her hand, tiny bits and parts of earth and dust surrounded me, hitting my fire as if a million bees were stinging me.

I tried to find my air inside of me, but I couldn't keep the fire up and blow away the dust at the same time. As the tiny particles were getting stronger and stronger, I pulled my fire back and exchanged it with air. Pushing against the particles, I let out a cry. I didn't know if the others could hear me, but I was hoping someone might come to check up on me and give me a hand.

"You don't have to scream." Sophia laughed. "This room is soundproof, and I made sure to close the door. No one will find you here."

"What do you want from me?" I blasted away the particles, my breathing ragged.

"Right now I want you to stop fighting me." Two branches tried to wrap themselves around my feet, and I stomped at them. Usually, earth elementals had to have a plant or a tree nearby to be able to control it, but Sophia seemed to be able to conjure it. A shimmering thread followed, but I broke through it with ease.

"My friends are not stupid. They'll find us." There was no way the others would just believe Sophia and I had disappeared, especially when they knew the truth.

"Keep telling yourself that." Sophia's air slammed into me, knocking my breath out of my chest. I wanted to summon my own air, but I couldn't focus on it. She lifted me up and pinned me against the wall, her air closing around my neck. I flailed my hands and feet, trying to force any of my elements out, but it wasn't working.

"Go to sleep, Moira. I want to familiarize myself with your body. You see, no one will know you're here, and I'll come out wearing your face. Tainteds will follow me and I'll bring all of them here. No one will be able to stop me."

The darkness clouded the edges of my vision.

Chapter 23

The whole building started to shake and I wasn't sure if I was imagining it or if it was real. But judging by the look on Sophia's face and the weakening grip of her element, it was all real. While she was distracted, I found my air inside of me and pushed her invisible threads away from my throat and body. I sank to the floor, creating a protective shield of air around me.

A loud banging came from the top of the stairs, and when a breeze whooshed inside, I knew the door had been opened. Sophia pursed her lips.

"Looks like we have company," she said. "Such a shame."

Before she could attack me again, I turned myself into air and rushed for the door. But as I emerged from Sophia's secret room, I found myself in the middle of yet another fight.

"Oh thank God you're here," Marissa said, holding up a wall of fire. "We're under attack."

"What?" I dodged a waterball and looked at the man dressed in black who was using his air against Kenna's. "Who are these people?"

"Sophia's supporters." Marissa grunted, backing away a few steps.

"When did they get here?" I doubted Sophia could have notified them that she'd be coming or that she needed help with me.

"A few minutes ago. There's at least ten of them."

"Are they regulars or tainteds?" Why would any tainted elemental work for Sophia? If they had been mind-controlled, I could fix that, and then we wouldn't have to fight them.

"No clue, but they keep using only one element."

"A little help here!" Ashley yelled, and I flew in front of her, pushing her down to the ground just in time to avoid a bunch of ice shards that were coming from behind her. I materialized and faced the woman, who was forming another ice shard in her hand. She suddenly raised her arms, and if I hadn't looked up and shielded my head with my fire, I would've been pierced by a huge stalactite.

"Don't hurt Moira! I need her!" I heard Sophia's voice, but I couldn't see her. Some of the equipment had been destroyed in the fight, and I nearly slipped on the nylon that was lying on the floor.

"There she is!" a male voice said, and two shimmering clouds rushed toward me. Turning myself into air, I whizzed past a box and headed for the exit. If only Sophia and her friend were tainteds, then I'd have to drag them away from the others, because the two of them were the most dangerous ones.

But as I landed on the hard, dusty ground in front of the building, I saw Sam and Kenna fighting three men in the fields. It seemed like the fight was going to continue outside, because after Sophia, the rest of the elementals came running, and Marissa and Ashley were after them, dodging elemental attacks and trying to get a hit on someone.

"You can't fight all of us," Sophia said, materializing in front of me. The second shimmering cloud turned into a man with curly dark hair. It was Terry.

"Those are just regulars, aren't they?" I nodded at the people who were now using fire and water to push Ashley away from them.

"Oh, it's not them you have to be afraid of," Sophia said. "Your tainteds are weak. I took your best already, and I'll take you too."

"No, you won't." I took a deep breath, my fingers curling into fists.

"We can end this fight right here and now." Sophia took a step closer, and a shimmering thread shot out of her and went toward my head. I turned into air and dodged it, then flew right through it to sever it.

"You think you're strong, but you're not." Sophia nodded at Terry, and two shimmering threads started for me. I avoided one, but the second one reached its target. I dropped to the ground, feeling as if my mind was being split in two.

As I covered my head with both hands, I squinted at Sophia and saw her approaching me. The shimmering thread embedded itself stronger into my mind, and I cried out. Focusing on my own element, I pushed against the intrusion with everything I had. Was I feeling the thread's pain worse than ever because I knew what it was trying to do to me?

One part of me wanted to stop fighting and just give Sophia whatever she wanted. Biting down on my lip so hard that I drew blood, I called to my fire and let it take over me. Every inch of me was turning into flames, and Sophia backed away, uncertainty flashing in her eyes.

"Help me out," she said to Terry, whose shimmering thread joined hers, but it couldn't breach my fire. I slowly lifted myself to my feet and advanced toward them. Every part of me was fire, and I didn't want to lose it because it seemed to be the only protection I had against Sophia's and Terry's elements. Moving was a bit difficult because my legs felt way too heavy and I wasn't quite sure where and how I was taking a step, but Sophia easily evaded my fiery fist that was going for her jaw.

"You don't think you can actually win this, do you? You might be able to protect yourself, but they can't." Sophia smirked, then looked at Terry. "Mind-control them to stop fighting."

He immediately went toward the others, and I fought the urge to smile. If my mind control worked, Terry would fail at his task. I didn't know how my friends would react to conflicting orders, but I hoped I had prevented any trouble with my careful choice of words.

"It's just you and me now," Sophia said as we circled each other. "Why don't you drop that ugly disguise so we can play?"

Opening my mouth was a strange sensation, as if someone was parting my flesh. "I don't want to play." I rushed her, but she got out of my way at the last moment.

"Something's wrong!" Terry yelled, and Sophia's face turned into a scowl.

"What did you do now, you incompetent fool?" she hissed.

"I mind-controlled them, but they aren't doing what..."

"Then you did it wrong. Do I have to do everything myself?" She blasted me back with her air before I could reach her. "Deal with her, but don't kill her."

"I'm not your dog," he snarled. "You can't just order me around..."

"Well, I can. You can't do anything right!" She threw her hands up, then turned invisible and headed toward Ashley and Marissa, who were holding up just fine against the attacks of ice, water, fire, air, and earth, probably because their opponents were just regular elementals.

Terry pressed his lips into a tight line as he faced me. "Show me what you got, girl."

"I don't have to show you anything. Looks like Sophia doesn't really hold you in high regard. I guess fighting you will be easy," I said, hoping to annoy him enough so that he'd be more careless.

"You don't know anything about me!" A huge wave of water appeared out of nowhere and threatened to fall on me, so I quickly raised an airy shield and slammed it into the wave, sending drops of water flying everywhere. It almost seemed as if it were raining. But some of the drops had reached Sophia's shimmering cloud, and she tumbled to the ground, her body flashing from invisible to visible. She clearly hadn't expected anything to hit her cloud and hadn't parted her air right.

Glad that she was struggling, I focused back on Terry, who was intently looking at something behind my back. Shit. I threw myself to the ground at the slightest touch of a breeze against the back of my neck, barely avoiding a hit from behind. But what I didn't expect was the huge watery snake that slithered across my body and started for my neck.

I screamed, breaking through the water with my air, but a powerful gust of wind lifted me up into the air and tossed me across the field. My shoulder painfully connected with the ground and a soft moan escaped my lips. As I rolled through the grass, I saw Sophia creating a big tornado in her rage. She must have failed to mind-control my friends. I pushed myself to my feet and ran toward the others, who were staring at the tornado with fearful eyes.

"Kenna!" I yelled. "Help me with this!"

Kenna's eyes met mine and she nodded. She was the only one who had air, and I doubted I could stop the tornado by myself since it was getting stronger with each second. I directed my element at the tornado, trying to swallow its energy and mix it with mine. Kenna did the same, focusing on the other side of the tornado so it was being held between our elements.

Marissa successfully knocked out two regular elementals, who started to flee when they saw the tornado. The rest of Sophia's supporters must have dispersed, because they were nowhere to be seen. They were clearly too afraid to face whatever would happen next.

"What do we do?" Sam asked. From the corner of my eye, I could see Terry coming toward us.

"Don't let him help her!" I yelled, increasing the strength of my element so the tornado shifted to Kenna's side a bit more, but Sophia's power wasn't getting any weaker.

Terry successfully sent Marissa, Ashley, and Sam flying and they landed not far from me, briefly distracting me. Terry joined his forces with Sophia, whose face was red with anger. The tornado grew even bigger, and strands of my hair ended up in my face. Shaking my head, I kept shoving my air at the tornado, but my attack didn't seem to have any effect on its strength.

"Marissa!" I said as she was pushing herself to her feet. We all had to step away because the tornado was threatening to swallow us into itself. Broken pieces of metal were already being sucked up into it, and I knew if that happened to one of us, we wouldn't get out alive.

"What?" Marissa shielded her eyes, her shirt flapping in the strong wind.

"I can't let go of this! Run to the other side with Sam and Ashley and attack Sophia and Terry." If we could unbalance or even distract Sophia and Terry, then we had a better chance of stopping this. Marissa nodded, then helped Sam get to his feet, and they all dashed across the field, careful not to get caught into the tornado that was shimmering with magic.

"It's too strong!" Kenna yelled. "We'll have to let it go!"

"We can't!" The elemental energy around the tornado was so powerful that I could feel its pressure on my face. Behind Terry, I could see a figure approaching, probably Marissa. She threw a log at Terry, who fell to his knees, his element leaving the tornado and slamming back into him. Sam was on him in a moment, punching and kicking. Sophia shrieked, the power of her element waning, and her body started to shake and shimmer.

The tornado slowed down, its size rapidly decreasing, as if someone had sucked it into an invisible hole. Kenna pulled her element back, and I let mine return to me too. Sophia slumped to the ground, her chest heaving. But as Marissa tried to approach her, Sophia jumped to her feet and hit the ground.

Everything started to shake and the earth parted under Sophia's fist. Marissa lost her balance, and the crack in the earth kept spreading while advancing toward us. Kenna and I immediately turned into air, lifting ourselves up and watching as a new tornado started to form from the ground. The ripple kept going, splitting the earth and guiding the tornado forward, right in the direction of the city.

"Stop it!" I yelled and rushed at Sophia. Materializing just before my body collided with hers, I slammed into her and we both rolled on the ground. Her hands briefly shimmered, and I climbed on top of her.

"Do you have those element-blocking cuffs?" I asked Ashley, who was trying to help Marissa up.

"Yeah," she said. "But I don't think they'll hold her."

"Then put all you've got on her. Quick. And on Terry too." When I was sure Sophia wasn't getting up, probably because she had exhausted most of her energy, I lifted myself up and dusted off my pants. She must have overestimated her abilities and thought she could just suck us up into her tornado.

"Um, we have a problem," Kenna said as Sam and Ashley were tying up Sophia and Terry with multiple element-blocking cuffs and bracelets.

I looked up at Kenna, my eyebrows shooting up. Then I noticed the huge thing behind her back. The tornado hadn't stopped. It was still advancing, tearing through the earth, yanking trees, and sucking up everything in its way. Shit. "We have to stop it!"

"How?" Kenna stared at me.

"I don't know, but we can't let it reach the city!" I didn't know if anyone would spot the tornado before it was too late and send forces to fight it, but I could still see the shimmering around the tornado, and I wasn't sure if the regular forces would be enough.

"We can't just leave them here..."

"Yes, we can!"

"But what about Nick and everyone else?" Kenna insisted.

"We'll question Sophia and Terry later. Come on!" No matter how much I wanted to find Jaiden, I had to stop the tornado first. Jaiden was probably being held somewhere in the city and if we let that tornado... A shudder ran through my body. No, I couldn't be thinking about that now.

When I was sure Sophia and Terry were properly tied up, I grabbed Ashley's and Sam's hands and turned them into air. Kenna took Marissa, and we were flying after the tornado. I hoped none of Sophia's supporters had stayed behind to help her, but there was no time to worry about that now. We had to stop this thing from destroying the city.

Chapter 24

"We're not going to make it!" Kenna yelled as we were getting closer to the tornado, but it was advancing too fast, and I could already see the outline of the city in front of us.

"Hurry up!" I increased my speed, trying to ignore the pressure that carrying Ashley and Marissa caused. I'd never flown this fast before. Kenna was a little behind, but I thought we could make it. The only question was what we would do to stop the damn thing. I zoomed past the tornado, feeling the tugging of its force, but I kept my distance because I didn't want to risk getting sucked in.

"Come on!" I plunged toward the ground. As soon as we all materialized, I focused on my air and directed it at the tornado that was swirling toward us. We were lucky there were only empty fields around here, but one glance over my shoulder told me we were way too close to the houses. If we didn't stop the tornado here, it would rip straight through people's homes.

"What do we do?" Kenna asked. "It's gotten stronger even without the help of Sophia's elements!"

"Use your air on it. We have to slow it down or at least keep it in place." I sent a powerful blast toward the tornado, wrapping my air around it. Kenna did the same, but the tornado cut right through our shimmering and advanced without a problem.

"Shit! It's not working!" Kenna stepped back.

"This isn't just air," I said, as the ground started to dangerously shake under my feet. "This thing is both air and earth."

"Should we try both of our elements then?" Kenna looked at me, frowning. "What if that only makes it stronger?"

"I don't know. We have to try." I found my fire inside of me and combined it with air, turning the fire blue. With a cry, I unleashed the mix on the tornado. A bright light resembling lightning cut through the tornado in the spot where my fire hit it.

"It's slower," Marissa noted.

"But it's still moving." And it wasn't getting any smaller either.

"Maybe we should all try using our elements on it," Sam said. "Even if we can just redirect it, it will be better than letting it pass through the city."

"Yeah, okay." We didn't really have many options, so we all sent our elements at the tornado. Kenna was using a bit of fire and then air, Marissa was exchanging fire and water, Ashley was mostly using earth because her mist was probably too weak, and Sam was trying to raise a barrier of earth to stop the tornado's progress.

"I think the problem is this isn't a regular tornado. It should've stopped by now." Sam gritted his teeth, his hair plastered to his forehead.

"I know." The tornado was getting slower, but it was still getting closer to us and if we didn't do something soon, it would pass right through us.

"What if we try to create a big wall? Would it bounce off it?" Ashley asked.

"I don't know. It could tear right through it, and I doubt we can just combine our elements since they're very likely to cancel each other out." Too bad our elements didn't seem to be strong enough to undo whatever Sophia had created. Her magic was way too powerful.

"If we could suck the energy out of it somehow…" Marissa said.

"What's that?" Sam's panicked voice made me tear my eyes from the tornado and focus on the shimmering behind my back.

"If Sophia and Terry freed themselves…" Ashley said.

"They wouldn't be coming from the direction of the city," I said, wondering who the newcomers were. They were certainly tainteds, but I didn't know if they were rushing to Sophia's aid or ours. When they materialized not far from us, I could see at least ten tainteds. I didn't recognize any of them. The wind was getting stronger, and my air wasn't providing enough of a barrier to stop the tornado.

"How can we help?" one of the tainteds asked. His black hair was cut short, his gray eyes focused on the tornado.

"Help? Oh thank God!" Marissa sighed in relief.

"Use your elements to stop this thing!" I yelled.

"Okay." The guy waved the others over and they all aligned with us. "What if we try raising multiple walls in front of it?"

"What do you mean? Our elements would cancel each other," I said.

"No, they wouldn't if we raise one wall after the other, like dominoes."

"And if the tornado brings them down like dominoes?" Kenna asked.

"Maybe it will, but that should slow it down enough. If we all just shoot our energy at it without thought, we could make it even stronger or cancel each other's attacks before they reach the tornado."

The guy had a point. Just because we couldn't see our elements canceling each other didn't mean that wasn't happening. And now there were more of us, so it would be harder to get everyone a clear area to hit, and by the time we agreed who'd do what, it could be too late. "Okay, let's do it."

"Good. Raise the walls of your strongest element," the guy said. "One by one. Starting from that end." He pointed at Sam.

"Let's hope it works." We all pulled our elements back, and Sam focused on creating the first wall. Ashley was next, her wall of earth positioned right behind Sam's, but not close enough to touch it. Everyone created their walls, and I made one out of blue fire. The guy's eyebrows shot up when he saw it, and he looked at me, a small smile tugging at his lips. The tornado was quickly approaching, and it cut through Sam's wall like a knife. Sam groaned in frustration, then his eyes widened as Ashley's wall went down too.

"Um, guys," a dark-haired girl said. "Were we expecting this to happen or should we run for cover?"

"Not yet, Emma," the guy said. "It won't stop immediately."

But as more walls fell, I tapped my foot against the ground, my stomach churning.

"You're a bit too confident about this, Spike," one of the tainteds yelled, but I couldn't see who it was because I didn't want to look away from the tornado.

"Shh, just give it time." Spike came to stand closer to me. I could feel his eyes on me, so I looked up at him. "You and I should create one final wall."

"How?" I frowned. All I'd seen him do was create a firewall, and that one had fallen too, so I didn't understand why only he and I should do it. Besides, our elements wouldn't be able to work with each other, unless we somehow kept them apart enough. Maybe that was what he meant. Maybe he could manipulate his element better, so there would be no risk of the elements touching.

"Use clean fire," he said. "And let it merge with mine."

"Merge with yours?" My eyebrows lifted in surprise. "I don't think that would work."

"It will."

He looked pretty confident about it. "I'm sorry, but... I doubt I can do that. I mean, I wasn't really merging my element..."

"Don't worry. You won't have to do anything. I can take care of everything, but I need your element."

If he meant he could swallow my element into his and then use it, then he was more than confident about his abilities. Just who did this guy think he was? Now wasn't the time to show off, and since we'd never fought together or tried this out, we couldn't know how our elements would react. "And what if my element defeats yours?"

"Doesn't matter. I can still take control of it."

"Hurry up," Kenna said. "This thing is about to go through the tenth wall."

The tornado was nowhere near stopping. "I..."

"We're cousins," Spike said, and I gaped at him. "From your father's side. That's why I can work with your fire easily."

It took me a moment to process that thought. I didn't know much about my biological father's family, but if Spike said we could do this... "Okay."

I let my fire surge out and focused on creating a wall almost as huge as the tornado itself. Spike's fire joined in, and I almost thought it would break through mine, but it didn't. The wall kept getting thicker and stronger as we both fed it with our energies.

"Everyone get out of the way!" I yelled, just in case our attempt failed. The others didn't have to risk their lives.

"Are you sure?" Marissa asked.

"Yes!" Spike and I yelled at the same time, and they immediately broke into a run while some turned into air.

"Watch out for the tornado if it changes direction," Spike said.

My heart was thudding loudly in my chest, sweat trickling down my back, but I kept feeding the wall.

"Marissa!" I yelled, just as the tornado went through the last wall and was heading toward Spike's and mine. "If something happens to me... find Jaiden and the others!"

"I will!" she yelled back, and a fraction of me relaxed. "But you'll beat this!"

"So, cousin," Spike said as if we were chatting over a coffee. "It's nice to finally meet you."

"Yeah, you too." Although I didn't know anything about him, so I wasn't sure yet.

I was barely breathing when the tornado collided with the wall. The heat and wind rushed around me, making it hard to concentrate, but I didn't stop fueling the wall with my energy. The tornado made a dent in the wall, stretching it out, but it didn't break through. At least not yet.

"Wrap the fire around it!" Spike said, and I did as he told me. The tornado was now a fiery tornado, but it was moving in place, as if caught in a net. "Take the energy back into yourself."

"What? But how?"

"Just imagine your energy returning back with your element."

"But..."

"No buts; do it!" Spike commanded, and I closed my eyes, allowing my energy to return to me and hoping this wouldn't unleash the tornado again. A strong gust of wind threw me back, and I opened my eyes. Shouts broke out in the field, and as I lifted myself up on my elbows, I noticed a big black hole in the ground, and the tornado was nowhere to be seen.

Spike was lying on his side and coughing. Other tainteds immediately appeared at his side, helping him up.

"We did it!" Marissa skipped toward me as I pushed myself to my feet. I could feel the energy inside of me, and I placed my hand over my chest, although I doubted the energy was actually there.

"What happened?" I asked as Marissa jumped around me.

"You and Spike sucked the tornado's energy into yourselves," she said.

"We did?" I made my way to Spike, who was high-fiving his friends, a broad smile on his face.

"Hey," he said to me. "It worked."

"Yeah, how did we... do that exactly?"

"The mix of our elements was stronger than the tornado, and we turned its energy into ours, so we could easily take it back."

"Thank God for that." I ran my hand through my tangled hair.

"Yeah, there was a high chance it wouldn't work or that the tornado would resist, but I'm glad it didn't," he said.

"Me too."

"At least we got our energy back." He offered me a smile.

"We have to go," Sam said. "Sophia and Terry could free themselves and..."

Spikes' eyes narrowed. "Sophia and Terry?"

"We have to go help our friends," I said, not willing to talk about this with strangers. Spike might be my cousin, but I didn't know anything about whose side he was on. Just because he had helped stop the tornado didn't mean he knew how it had been created or by whom.

"Can we help?" Spike asked.

"No, that won't be necessary," I said quickly.

"Where did that thing come from?" Emma asked.

"Yeah, who created that? It had to be an elemental." Spike searched my eyes, but I wiped all emotion off my face and just smiled at him.

"We'll figure it out."

"Someone's coming!" Ashley yelled, and I heard the distinct sound of helicopters and sirens. The cops were coming here. It was time for us to leave.

"We really have to go now." I said. "Thank you for your help. We couldn't have done it without you."

"Okay, good luck to you, cousin. I'll deal with the cops and the press." He inclined his head to me. With a smile, I rushed toward Kenna, who was already turning into air with Ashley. Grabbing Sam and Marissa, I let my air envelop us all and rose into the sky.

Chapter 25

I breathed out a sigh of relief when I saw Sophia and Terry still sitting on the ground. They were struggling against the bracelets and cuffs we'd put on them. Sophia sneered at me when I approached.

"You won't get away with this," she yelled. "If you kill me, the whole world will be after you!"

"Tell me where you took my friends." I crouched in front of her.

"They're dead!" she spat out.

My hand shot out and wrapped itself around her throat. Sophia's eyes widened. "Tell me where they are or I swear to God there won't be enough pieces of you left for the cops to identify." I didn't plan to hurt her too much, let alone kill her, but she didn't have to know that. "And you'll be next." I shot a glare at Terry, who visibly swallowed.

"Just tell her!" Terry blurted out.

"No, she can go to..." Sophia's words were cut off as I squeezed harder.

"Tell me!" I said through my teeth.

"Okay, okay!" she finally whispered, and I let go of her.

"I'm waiting," I said, as she coughed.

"They're in an old shack near Howell Park. You can't miss it," she said, and something flashed through her eyes. I doubted she'd lie to me, but I had a feeling someone was guarding that shack, and she thought she'd be sending me into a trap.

"See? That wasn't hard." I got to my feet, and turned toward Marissa. "Call the cops."

"What?" Marissa frowned. "Are you sure we...?"

"Yeah, call the cops." Sophia bobbed her head. Poor Sophia. She thought the cops would come here and free her, and she'd spin some story about how evil tainted elementals had kidnapped and threatened her. I took Marissa by the arm and pulled her aside so that Sophia and Terry couldn't overhear us.

"My camera is still working." I glanced down at tiny thing on my shirt. Thank God these things are element-proof and resistant to pretty much anything. "I think."

"Mine fell off." Marissa grimaced.

"Doesn't matter. We should have enough proof against Sophia on this." I detached the camera and handed it to Marissa. "Check the others and get the footage. Then send Ashley or Sam to put it up on the Internet before you call the cops. If they were mind-controlled to destroy all evidence against Sophia or are working for her, this should be enough to protect us."

"Wait, aren't we going to get Noah and the others?" Marissa tilted her head.

"Yeah, we are, but only Kenna and me. We can deal with Sophia's guards quietly, and I don't think we can carry all of you with us to the other end of the city."

"Oh, okay." Marissa's face fell, so I placed my hand on her shoulder. "You stay here and make sure those two don't escape, and be careful."

"What if the cops try to arrest me?" she asked.

"I don't think they will, but if they do, I'll come for you, okay? If you see they are hostile and are planning to attack you, run like hell. Do you think you can do that?"

"Yeah." She offered me a small smile.

"Good." I really hoped Sophia hadn't mind-controlled all the cops in the city, but maybe she hadn't bothered since she could change shapes. Maybe her mind control wasn't as strong as her other abilities. "Just make sure the cops know what they're dealing with."

I wondered how the trial would proceed if Sophia took on someone else's likeness, but I supposed her elements could be used to identify her since she couldn't change them.

"Kenna!" I yelled, and she looked at me in annoyance. "We're going to get your brother and the others."

Her face immediately lit up and she turned into air.

"Follow me." I let my air consume me and surged up. *Hang on, Jaiden. I'm coming.*

Kenna and I materialized not far from the shack Sophia had mentioned. There were no windows, and the door was closed.

"Do you think they're really here?" Kenna asked.

"Probably. Sophia knows we'd come back for her if they weren't," I said. "But there are probably guards inside or maybe element-blockers." I wasn't sure how they were keeping Jaiden, Noah, and Nick in there because they were all very powerful. And together, they would've blown up this small shack ages ago. Unless something was hiding behind the innocent-looking walls.

"I could fly around and see if there's a hole I can squeeze through." Kenna eyed the shack.

"Okay, do it, but come back." From my hiding spot behind the thick bushes, I could easily blast anyone who dared attack Kenna. She whooshed past me and headed for the shack. Nothing moved. Maybe the guards were all inside.

My stomach did a nervous flip at the thought that they might have transferred Jaiden and the others somewhere else when they hadn't heard back from Sophia, but as long as everyone was still alive... My mouth was dry, and I blinked, trying to clear my thoughts. Kenna landed next to me.

"I couldn't see much, but there's a tiny hole in the wall. At least two guards with weapons are in there. Whatever protection they have, it might be inside."

"Okay." I called to my air. "Then let's see if we can get them out."

"How?" Kenna asked, then saw my shimmering thread. "Oh."

"Where's the hole?" I asked.

"Right there, under the roof," she said. I let my air feel the wood and slip through the hole. Maybe I couldn't see who was inside, but I could try to get into someone's head. And if someone severed my thread and could see my shimmering, then we'd know we were dealing with people like us. My air roamed through the space, and I guided it forward, unsure if I would be able to actually sense someone's mind or I'd have to brush against it with my air first to be able to tell it was there.

"Anything?" Kenna asked after a while.

"Not yet. I hope I won't slip into the mind of one of our own." Although that might not be a bad idea after all, because if they were unconscious, maybe I could wake them up.

"What if they're not in there?" Kenna worried her lower lip.

I raised my finger to shush her, and lifted my air a bit higher. Something collided against it, and I waited for a moment, then let it crawl over the thing. An image of white brain signals flashed in my mind, and I felt myself smile.

"Open the door and come out," I whispered so my thoughts would stay clear. I didn't want to risk losing control or messing something up, especially when my target was so far away. A couple of moments later, an armed man in military clothes walked out, opening the door wide.

"Hey, what are you doing?" another man rushed after him. "We're not supposed to go outside!"

"I heard something. Let's check it out." I forced the guy whose mind I was controlling to say exactly what I wanted him to.

"Heard what?" The other one snapped his fingers. "What are you talking ab... Shit!"

"They figured it out!" Kenna yelled. "Let's go before they close the door."

I nodded, pulling out of the man's brain, and followed Kenna. We whooshed into the shack just before the men closed the door.

"It's one of them!" a man yelled, his voice filled with panic. "They're here!"

"I don't see anything!" another one said.

"Of course you don't, you dumbass, they're tainteds."

"Oh shit. Oh shit. She told us they wouldn't be coming!" The first one sat behind a computer, pressing a button. "They're here! The energy is spiking!"

"What if it's yours? You're freaking out like a little girl."

"It's not mine. I swear."

"Look at him. He's sweating."

"What? It's hot in here."

Kenna and I pressed ourselves against the wall, flying low, although I doubted these men would see us even if we appeared right in front of their eyes. They weren't like us. Kenna's shimmering finger waved toward the part of the room hidden by a white curtain. We slipped underneath it, and as we rose up, my invisible heart skipped a beat. Jaiden, Nick, and Noah were lying on metal beds, their arms and legs tied, their eyes closed. Kenna immediately materialized next to her brother and placed her hands on his face.

"Nick, it's me. Wake up!" she whispered.

I watched Jaiden's serene face and started undoing the binds, my hands slightly shaking from both relief and the desire to get Jaiden and the others out of here as soon as possible.

"They're in here!" The curtain was pulled back and more shouts followed. I let go of Jaiden and blasted the first man who approached me with my air. Someone fired and I swallowed the bullets into my fire.

"Can you take them with you?" I asked Kenna, who was quickly freeing Noah.

"I'll take my brother. You carry Jaiden and Noah," she said. "I can't carry two."

"Okay. Go!" I watched her as she turned herself and her brother into air and flew past the men, who weren't even able to see her. Sophia clearly hadn't expected anyone to get the location out of her, and since Terry hadn't blurted it out immediately, that meant she had been the only one who knew. Of course, finding other tainteds and getting them to watch over Jaiden and the others would've been difficult and might have caused spikes of energy that were too big.

I sent two gusts of air at the guards, sending them flying and knocking the weapons out of their hands. Grabbing Jaiden's and Noah's arms, I turned us all into air and zoomed out of the shack before anyone could react. I could see Kenna's shimmering in front of me, so I went after her. When she lowered herself into one of the alleys, I knew she was going for the lab.

Once we got inside, I lowered Noah and Jaiden on the beds. Kenna had materialized her brother on the sofa, but his eyes were still closed.

"What's wrong with them?" Kenna's voice was high-pitched.

"I guess they're asleep." Their breathing seemed regular and they didn't have any visible injuries.

"When are they going to wake up?" She paced up and down the room.

"I don't know." I rubbed my arms. "We should check what the others…"

"We can text them to come here if they didn't get in trouble."

"Okay. Do it." I was sure Kenna needed something to occupy herself with. She immediately went to find a phone.

"Jaiden, can you hear me?" I said softly, placing my hand over his, but he didn't even stir.

"The others are on their way here," Kenna said when she returned. "And surprise, surprise. They weren't arrested. The cops only took Sophia and Terry."

My eyebrows shot up. That was indeed a surprise. "Turn on the TV. Maybe there's something on the news." The press was probably going wild about the tornado, and if they heard Sophia had been arrested, they'd be all over that too.

"Are you sure this thing still works?" Kenna stepped in front of a tiny old TV that had a layer of dust on it.

I shrugged. "Try it."

She pressed a button, and something like a pop could be heard. The screen flickered, but a few moments later it cleared, and we could see the reporter. Kenna fiddled with two buttons, and the reporter's voice became audible.

"According to the latest reports, Sophia Mornell and her partner, Terry Garrly, have been arrested for multiple crimes, including the creation of a big tornado that was threatening the city. It appears that Ms. Mornell is a tainted elemental herself. We aren't exactly sure how that is possible, considering her age, but we should find out more once the official statement is released," the woman said. "Take a look at the newest footage."

A video of Sophia and Terry being led into a silver truck appeared on the screen.

"Is that an element-blocking truck?" Kenna asked.

"Yeah, I guess the cops don't want to risk Sophia escaping."

"Do you think she could?"

"Even if she does, she won't be able to continue her campaign." Well, not unless she became someone else.

The reporter reappeared on the screen. "There have been multiple reports about tainted elementals who helped stop the tornado. We've obtained some footage that seems to confirm that rumor."

As soon as I saw Jaiden turn into Sophia, I realized the video was from my camera. A slow smile appeared on my lips. There was no way she could pretend that she wasn't one of us. And if we wanted to, we could even pin our crimes on her, since there was absolutely no way to prove that she hadn't pretended to be one of us before. I knew she had to familiarize herself with the person whose appearance she wanted to steal, but how would she demonstrate that? Still, I was glad she had been caught, and I wasn't about to let her answer for what I'd done.

A soft moan turned my attention to Jaiden, who mumbled something.

"Jaiden?" I was immediately next to him.

His eyes slowly opened, and he blinked at me. Then he sat up so fast that I had to step back. He stared at me, breathing hard. "Is it really you?" he asked.

"Yeah. Sophia and Terry have been caught." I moved away so he could see the TV screen behind my back.

His shoulders slumped and he sighed in relief.

"Are you feeling okay?" I asked tentatively, my pulse racing.

"I... yeah." He settled back on the pillows, and I couldn't hold myself back anymore. I hurled myself into his arms, tears welling up in my eyes. Every emotion I'd kept buried deep inside me came out all at once, and I crushed Jaiden's mouth with mine. He kissed me back with all the passion in the world.

As I pulled back and wiped away my tears, Jaiden smiled at me and reached out for my hand, then glanced at Noah and Nick. "They're still out?"

"Yeah. Do you know what she gave you? How did she even get to you?"

"I don't know. A sedative, I guess." He scratched his eyebrow. "In that mansion... I was preparing myself to fight those devices when something stabbed me in the neck and everything went black."

Noah stirred too, and Nick groaned. Someone must have been giving them the sedatives at the same hour, and now that Nick and Noah hadn't gotten the next dose, they were waking up too. Kenna's face lit up as she pulled her brother into a hug.

"How did you do that?" Jaiden was frowning at the TV screen. "There was a tornado?"

"Yeah, I'll tell you all about it." I grinned, and let go of him so I could go check on Noah.

"Hey," I said softly.

"Moira?" His brow furrowed. "Where am I...?"

"Back at the lab. Sophia has been caught."

"Oh?" He blinked. "Where's Tiffany?"

"Who's Tiffany?" I couldn't remember anyone with that name.

"My friend from high school. She picked me up when I was..." He bit down on his lip.

I grimaced. "That wasn't your friend. It turned out Sophia and Terry can change into other people."

"What?" Jaiden and Noah said at the same time, and Nick just stared at me as if I had grown another head.

"Long story. We'll explain." I waved my hand and faced Nick. "How did they take you?"

"Noah came for me." He frowned.

"No, I didn't," Noah said.

"Oh, great." Nick ran his hand over his face. "So I fell for fake Noah."

"If Moira hadn't realized a fake Jaiden was with us, we wouldn't have..." Kenna started to say and Jaiden's head snapped toward me.

"Excuse me?" he said. "A fake Jaiden? What did…"

I raised my finger. "Let's start from the beginning…" And I launched myself into a difficult explanation of what they had all missed.

Chapter 26

I leaned my head on Jaiden's shoulder as I watched the TV screen. After a long and difficult trial, Sophia and Terry were sentenced to life in prison, not just for starting a dangerous tornado that could've killed many and destroyed the city, but also for rousing the public against tainteds, kidnapping and imprisonment, and manipulation of others with her elements.

The judge also decided to put Jaiden and me on some kind of probation because our crimes had been committed under difficult circumstances and because we'd done so much to help everyone. We could still go wherever we wanted and do whatever we wanted, but if we made a wrong move, we'd be sent to a special, well-protected prison too.

"It's finally over," Marissa sighed. We were all sitting around a big table at our new place. Now that we no longer had to run from Sophia or the cops, we could easily start our group to help tainteds. In fact, I'd used my grandfather's money to buy an old hotel and turned it into a safe haven for tainted elementals, who, for whatever reason, needed a place to stay.

"Yeah, it's over," Noah said. "But that's not the most important news today."

"It's not?" Ashley leaned forward.

"No. Since I'm officially the leader of this organization," Noah straightened his back and lifted his chin up, "I've been contacted by the government about their latest decision."

"And that is?" I raised an eyebrow at him.

"The government decided that tainteds will have equal rights as any other person on this planet." His lips spread into a smile. "Nobody can hunt us down or discriminate against us. Of course, the bad guys will be dealt with and treated like any other criminal."

"Why hasn't there been an official statement yet?" Jaiden asked.

"There is. Look!" Sam pointed at the TV screen and we all focused on the president as he said exactly what Noah had told us.

"But that's not all," the president said. "We will continue genetic manipulation because we think tainted elementals are our future, but any experiments on adults in an attempt to give them similar abilities are strictly forbidden."

"Wow," Marissa said. "Now we're important."

"Shh," Kenna hissed.

The reporter appeared on the screen, a smile on her face. "Wonderful news for the country and the whole world. I'm sure other governments will make a similar decision, although they don't have as many tainteds as we do. The president asked the representative of tainteds, Noah Boine, if the term tainted should be changed, but Mr. Boine said that it wouldn't be necessary because tainteds are very proud of who they are."

"Damn straight we are," Nick said, lifting his glass.

"But there's also some good news for the minority who didn't welcome this decision about tainteds' rights. Mr. Zali here has a very interesting project." The reporter stepped aside and a tall man with short light brown hair and blue eyes came into view. "Can you tell our viewers more about your project?"

"Sure. I'm developing a device that will be able to block mind control or any attempt of an elemental attack on a person's mind," Zali said proudly. "The beta testing should begin in two months."

"Wow, that sounds like a very useful device," the reporter said.

"It will be, but that's not all. We're also going to build sophisticated trackers and detectors," he said. "We'll ensure everyone feels safe in their homes or anywhere else... including tainted elementals, of course."

"That's wonderful news, Mr. Zali. We're looking forward to more of your inventions."

Jaiden's body stiffened, so I looked up at him.

"What's wrong?" I asked. "Are you worried someone might come after us? Now we can actually call the cops or anyone we want for help."

"No, it's not that. I know that guy. He used to work for my father," Jaiden said.

"Jack is going to be pissed." I had to stifle laughter. After Sophia's trial and ours, Jack had become the most wanted person in the country, mostly because he had experimented on adults and turned them into twisted versions of tainted elementals, and also because he was behind the murders Jaiden had committed for him. Still, Jack was very good at escaping and no one had found him. Yet.

Not that I cared much if he got caught, because a few days after Sophia had been arrested, Jaiden and I had gone to Jack's secret lab and found it empty, but there was one dose of Jaiden's serum and a note in which Jack commended us for good work with Sophia. I'd handed the serum over to my mom, and I was hoping she'd find a way to recreate it or find someone who could. It would be really annoying if we had to track down Jack to get the rest of it. But Jaiden was still fine, so I assumed we had some time.

"So did they ever find out what Sophia's big plan was?" Marissa asked. "I mean, she wouldn't have gone through all that trouble just to become the mayor or something."

"We don't know," I said. "She didn't want to say anything about that."

"What about her supporters?" Nick asked. "Are they still out there?"

"Probably." There was no way the cops had found all of them, and most claimed they had been mind-controlled, although I wasn't sure how much truth there was to that. "We should always be careful and watch out for crazy people."

"So everything stays the same?" Nick laughed. "I was actually attacked once when no one knew I was a tainted elemental."

"Really? Why?" Marissa asked.

Nick shrugged. "I don't know. I guess they thought I had an expensive phone they could steal and sell somewhere."

A bell rang, making me jump.

"That's our pizza." Ashley clapped her hands.

On the small screen of the intercom, I could see the delivery guy waiting in front of the door with a stack of boxes.

"Where's that button to open the main door?" Noah tapped his jacket for the device. "Oh, here."

Suddenly the boxes and the guy vanished, and we all gasped, except Noah, who grinned.

"Close your mouths, guys. It's the Tainted Delivery," he said. A shimmering cloud whooshed into the room and spread over the table. A couple of moments later, the guy materialized next to the table, and the boxes were neatly placed in front of us.

"That was quick," Noah said as he handed the money to the guy. "Keep the change."

"Thank you." The guy turned into a shimmering cloud and flew out.

"I hope the pizza isn't invisible," Nick said, reaching for one of the boxes. But as he opened it, he closed his eyes and breathed in the delicious scent of cheese and tomato. "Mmm, it's so damn real."

I opened the box nearest to me and grabbed a slice.

"I think people will start to like us real soon," Nick said as he chewed. "Who wouldn't want faster delivery? And we can carry more things with us if we turn them into air."

Kenna rolled her eyes. "Yeah, we get it, Nick. Stop eating like a pig and close your mouth."

He pouted and grabbed another slice of pizza.

"Wait, if everything is being taken care of and Noah is the leader, does that mean we can go on a vacation?" Jaiden's eyes met mine.

"A vacation?" I grinned. "Sounds like a good idea. Where would we go?"

"I don't know. Anywhere." He shrugged. "I haven't really done that before, so..."

"Oh, I have a whole list of places I want to visit."
"You do?"

"Yeah, don't you?" I frowned.

"I haven't thought about it at all."

"Well, you can make one." I punched him lightly on the shoulder. "Or we can just choose from my list, but we might have to get a map or something, because I've probably included every single country on the planet."

His eyes widened and he lifted his hands up. "Whoa, slow down. We're not going on a tour around the world."

"Why not?" I pouted. "We could go on a cruise and visit awesome places…" I looked up at him. "Do you like ships? If that bothers you, we can figure something else out."

"We'll think about it." He flashed me a smile.

"Good." I focused back on my food. I could use a vacation. A really long one.

Chapter 27

"I told you we should've gotten a map and just randomly pointed at a place," I said as Jaiden and I crossed the street. We'd been trying to find a good place to visit for days, but we still hadn't made up our minds. I wanted to go to another continent, and Jaiden preferred to go to another city across the country.

"We can still do that," he said, snaking his arm around my waist and pulling me to a stop in front of a restaurant. Bending his head, he lowered his lips to mine. "Actually, I don't care where I go, as long as I'm with you."

"Does that mean I get to choose?" I grinned.

"Yeah." He pressed his mouth against mine, his tongue parting my lips. I wrapped my arms around his neck.

"We should probably go inside." I glanced at the restaurant and stepped back from him. "We don't want to leave people waiting."

"We should've sent Noah to meet them."

"Totally, but they wanted us, so..." I tapped his nose with my finger. "We're going in."

"Fine." He pressed his lips together, but amusement flashed in his eyes. Two days ago, some tainted elementals had called me and requested for Jaiden and me to meet with them. They said they didn't want to talk to Noah because they believed we could be of more help. When I asked what they needed us for, they refused to say over the phone.

Jaiden thought it could be those tainteds who had escaped from Elemontera and were in hiding, so maybe they wanted to talk to us because we had experience with the cops about the whole Elemontera thing. I'd been suspicious, but they agreed to meet us in a public place, so I figured there wouldn't be any trouble.

Jaiden pushed the door open for me, and I stepped inside. A couple was sitting at one of the tables, eating and chatting. Only one more table was occupied, and I could see four figures with their backs turned to us.

"Are you sure we've got the right place?" Jaiden asked.

"I guess." I started toward the door that was leading to the kitchen, hoping to find a waiter who could tell me if someone was waiting for us, but as I made my way across the room, the lights went out.

I stopped, waiting for the lights to come back on. People stopped talking, and I heard the scraping of chairs and clinks of plates, but I didn't hear anyone complaining or asking what was going on.

"Jaiden?" I whispered, just as the lights returned, brighter than before, and I had to squint to be able to see. The whole room was glowing with yellowish light and I stumbled back, bumping into Jaiden. The people who'd been sitting were now on their feet, their faces serious and turned toward us.

"Let's go," I said softly, tugging at Jaiden's jacket, but a pressure in my chest made me pause. My limbs were suddenly heavy, my head spinning. What was going on? I tried to move, but I couldn't. As I searched for my elements inside of me, I realized I couldn't even feel them.

"You can stop trying," a dark-haired woman stepped forward, her red lips pulling into a smile. "You can't move or escape from here."

I gritted my teeth and moved my head toward the door, but I could see through the glass that something metallic had been pulled over it. No one would be able to see us if we tried to signal for help. "Who are you? What do you want?"

"How rude of me. I'm Tamara," the woman said. "As for what I want... well, just your energy."

"What?" I stared at her.

"Now that we've got the two of you, Sophia's sacrifice won't be for nothing."

"Sophia's sacrifice?" So these people were working with Sophia, but what did they want with us? Revenge?

"Yes, she went to prison and didn't reveal anything about our plan." Tamara came closer, but no matter how much I tried, I couldn't move or get my elements to work.

"What plan?" Jaiden said, his body twitching, but he couldn't do anything either.

"I doubt people like you pay attention to real issues in our world," she said. "But we're running out of water and energy. That's why the government wants to continue breeding elementals like you, but by the time you all grow up, it'll be too late. You have way too much elemental energy that you don't really need, so we came up with a powerful collector that will harness that energy and turn it into what our world really needs."

"What's wrong with you?" I said. "You could just adjust element collectors…"

"No, you don't understand. Taking such little amount of energy won't do. We need it all. Every last bit of it." Tamara's eyes flashed dangerously. "The only reason the government hasn't gone forward with this is because they consider it cruel and inhumane, but we have no such concerns. It's such a shame Sophia's plan was progressing too slowly, because now we can't use her abilities when we present our project to the government, but we'll find a way…"

"You're monsters," I spat.

"Call us whatever you want," Tamara said. "But I have your group to thank for being able to test our wonderful inventions." She spread her arms and pointed at the yellowish light.

"That mansion..." I started to say.

"Yeah, yeah. We were testing your energy and our systems. As you can see, we've made this one perfect and this time you won't be able to escape, no matter what you do. Our system recognizes your elements."

I swallowed hard. So they were planning to drain us of our elements or perhaps milk our elements until there was nothing left and turn them into electricity? Since neither Jaiden nor I had a water element, she couldn't really turn it into water... or maybe she could.

"It's not going to work," I said. "Jaiden's elements are artificial, and mine have been experimented on, so they're not pure. They can't be. You need pure elements for what you want."

"Ah, that's where you're wrong. All tainteds have pure elements, no matter how they've gotten them. It's funny. You're proud to call yourselves tainted, but your elements are the purest they could be. Having such elements is mankind's biggest dream. And when I take that precious energy from you... we could power up at least ten cities for two years."

"You're not going to get away with this!" I said. "The whole city knows us. They'll be looking for us."

"Doesn't mean that they'll find you, especially if you're no longer in this country." Tamara inclined her head toward one of the men standing behind her and he raised a gun. Two darts shot out of it when he pulled the trigger. One hit me in the arm, and as I glanced down, I could see green liquid draining out of it. My eyelids became heavy, and Tamara's face was becoming blurry until everything disappeared from view.

###

TAINTED ELEMENTS SERIES
DIFFERENT
INVISIBLE
MONSTER
CAPTIVE
HUNTED
RESILIENT

Also by Alycia Linwood

HUMAN

ELEMENT PRESERVERS SERIES

DANGEROUS
RUNAWAY
DIVIDED
NO ONE
RESTLESS
INDESTRUCTIBLE

More information:
www.alycialinwood.weebly.com